Praise for
Sloan Parker's Other Books

"Sloan Parker is an amazing writer. Her work is beautiful and touching and emotional. If you haven't read any of her books, I suggest you run out and do so!"

—Sadonna at The Armchair Reader

"...I have loved every one of Sloan Parker's books and this one is no different. ...exciting, suspenseful and most importantly, romantic. The love story between Walter and Kevin is so sweet and real. They have a connection that can't be denied by either one of them."

—Literary Nook on HOW TO SAVE A LIFE

"...a smoothly flowing plot that has enough angst, obstacles, and mystery to keep you glued from the first page to the last... I thoroughly enjoyed reading this fascinating and enthralling book and would definitely recommend it to anyone looking for a fantastic read that is worth every minute spent on it."

—Trish at Mrs. Condit Reads Books on HOW TO SAVE A LIFE

"...a beautiful love story... You can't help but fall in love with Linc and Jay. I can't recommend it enough. I can't wait to read more books by this author."

—Caroline at Book Lovers Inc. on BREATHE

"...an incredibly poignant story where the emotions are profoundly moving, the characterization is perfect, and the suspense is riveting."

— Nannette at Joyfully Reviewed on BREATHE

"...an emotional and sensual blockbuster."

—Joyfully Reviewed on MORE

OTHER TITLES BY SLOAN PARKER

MORE series
More (More Book 1)
More Than Most (More Book 2)

THE HAVEN series
How to Save a Life (The Haven Book 1)

Single Titles
Breathe
Take Me Home
More Than Just a Good Book
Something to Believe In
Friends and Lovers
The Break-In
Swept Away
A Lesson in Truth

I Swear to You

SLOAN PARKER

I SWEAR TO YOU
Copyright © 2014 by Sloan Parker

First Print Edition: 2017
Originally released in e-book format in 2014

ISBN-13: 978-1942517917
ISBN-10: 1942517912

Cover design by Lou Harper © 2016

This is a work of fiction. The names, characters, and incidents are either the product of the author's imagination or have been used fictitiously. Any resemblance to actual persons or incidents are coincidental.

Published by
Sloan Parker Press
www.sloanparker.com

I Swear to You

Prologue

Grady turned his pickup truck onto the narrow dirt driveway and glanced over at his roommate in the passenger seat. The side of Mateo's dark head was plastered against the window, his eyes closed, lips parted in sleep.

"This sucks," Grady whispered under his breath. He so didn't want to wake him.

It had been one hell of a shitty day, and Mateo deserved at least another hour or two of the ignorant bliss that came with sleep.

Grady sighed and tapped Mateo's thigh with the side of his fist. "We're here."

Mateo flinched awake, banging his elbow on the armrest as he bolted upright. That had to feel damn near perfect after what he'd gone through a little over an hour ago.

"Sorry, man."

Mateo blinked and shook his head as if to say it was fine.

He had drifted off halfway through the drive to Crystal Spring Lake, which was situated in the middle of forestland and farm country, fifty-five miles from their university in West Clinton, Ohio.

It had been pushing midnight by the time they'd left their dorm room, tossing some clothes and shit into their bags, heading out without telling any of their frat brothers or hockey teammates where they were going.

Or why.

As the truck came to a stop, Mateo nodded toward the north end of the property. "The guesthouse?"

"You know it."

It was odd that he'd asked. They always stayed in the one-room, pale-blue house that sat off to the side of the main cottage.

Maybe what he'd witnessed earlier had him feeling even more out of sorts than Grady had expected.

And why not? No matter what a guy felt about the girl he was seeing, when he caught her in bed with another guy, it fucking stung.

Mateo wrenched open the passenger door and got out.

Grady followed suit. Despite how warm it had been that day for early May, it was frigid at the lake at this time of night. Good thing he'd had the sense to grab their coats on their way out an hour earlier. Mateo hadn't been thinking too clearly when he'd stormed into their dorm room after catching his girl with a freshman from their hockey team, the guy's dick buried inside her.

Mateo paused in front of the truck like he was too exhausted to move another inch. He stared at the guesthouse, then out over the moonlit water.

The lake was just a speck on any map, and the nearest neighbor was a quarter mile away through the dense forest. Only a dozen houses sat around the perimeter of the lake. The two that Grady's family had owned all his life weren't anything elaborate, but it felt good to be away from school, to inhale the clear, crisp air, and stand in the piercing quiet.

With the moon barely a sliver of light in the sky, it was like they'd stepped into another world.

Maybe Mateo felt the same. He inhaled deeply like he was able to really breathe for the first time since they'd left the city, and then he walked to the shoreline and continued to stare out at the dark, still water.

Grady grabbed their bags and the case of beer and set everything on the porch of the guesthouse, then headed down to the shore. They stood almost shoulder to shoulder in the sand, though Mateo was a touch taller. They had the same dark hair, but in contrast to Mateo's darker skin, Grady's paler complexion always freckled easily in the sun.

The cool breeze picked up, blew across the surface of the

lake, and smacked into them. Mateo closed his eyes and lifted his face into the wind. With his hair swept back off his forehead, he looked like he did whenever he peeled off his helmet after a game, his black hair sweaty and slicked back.

His voice was low when he finally spoke. "Grady?"

"Yeah."

He waved that off like he'd changed his mind on what he'd been about to bring up. "Let's take the boat out."

"Sure. Let me go grab the key from the house."

"No." He shook his head again. "We fire up the motor this late, and the neighbors across the way will be bitching your dad out." With a tilt of his head, he gestured to the back of the property. "The canoe."

Grady looked toward the shed that sat behind the main house where the canoe and oars were stored. He shrugged. "Okay." It didn't matter that they'd probably come close to freezing their asses off out on the water. If this was what Mateo needed, Grady would do it. He'd row through a blizzard for Mateo.

They'd been coming out to the lake since they'd met in the first grade. All through school they'd spent their weekends there, hiking through the woods looking for tree frogs, and doing cannonballs off the dock to see who could make the biggest splash. In high school they'd progressed to taking either the canoe or the motorboat out on the lake and talking about which girls they wanted to fuck. They'd even moved to the guesthouse during the first three summers in college, both of them working part-time at the honky-tonk joint about a mile away. Grady knew Mateo had nowhere else to go. Asking his aunt and uncle if he could stay with them wasn't an option.

"They're just gonna say no."

He'd lived with them since he was three months old, but the minute he'd left for college, they'd practically forgotten he'd existed.

Fuck 'em.

Grady had made a point of telling Mateo he didn't need them. He had Grady's family. Hell, Grady's parents had done more for Mateo during one season of hockey—buying his gear and driving him to practice—than his aunt and uncle had ever bothered to do.

Without another word, they headed for the shed. It wasn't long before they had the canoe launched and were rowing away from the cottage, Grady seated in the bow and Mateo behind him in the stern. In the center of the lake, they stopped and let the canoe drift on the nearly still water.

There were no sounds of traffic, no guys bitching at each other, no blaring video games. Just the sporadic hoot of an owl in the distance.

Grady swung around to sit facing the back of the canoe. Mateo hadn't taken his eyes off the water.

"Fuck her," Grady said as he pulled out two beers. "Who needs her?"

Mateo nodded but said nothing.

Grady twisted open one of the beers and handed it to him, then opened his own. He guzzled it down, not knowing what to say or do.

He never felt this uncomfortable around Mateo. Then again, they didn't spend their days talking about this kind of thing.

Not that shit didn't ever get serious. Sometimes late at night in their dorm room, after a party, when they were both drunk, they'd talk about stuff they had never talked about with anyone else, that they'd only admit because they were alone, drunk, whispering in the dark. It was then that Mateo would admit how scared he was he'd fuck up in school and ruin his one chance to make something of himself, to prove to his aunt and uncle they were wrong about him. And maybe to prove to himself he could do it.

Grady hadn't known what to say to that. He had tried to tell Mateo his aunt and uncle didn't know crap about him, but he'd never gotten through.

Or maybe he had. Maybe Mateo needed those words from Grady, and that was why he'd brought it up in the first place.

And now, sitting in the canoe, Grady was yet again at a loss for what to say, for what Mateo needed him to say. So he drank his beer and waited.

Eventually Mateo looked away from the water and stared

down the mouth of his beer bottle. "I just finished reading this book about the psychology of introverts."

"Yeah?"

That wasn't a surprise. Mateo was always reading like he was on a deadline. Yet it wasn't just what was assigned for his classes. He devoured books the way the guys at the frat house inhaled pizza.

He also kept to himself a lot. He rarely said more than two consecutive sentences to anyone—except Grady.

It was that quiet, mysterious thing he had going on that girls found irresistible, thinking they could be the ones to get him to open up. He didn't even need the two sentences to get most girls in bed with him. He'd just flash them those serious dark eyes, and they were all over him.

Of course, it also could've been the story of how he'd gotten to Ohio from Mexico that did the girls in. Most people on campus had heard the rumor that Mateo was the famous "miracle baby." At three months old he'd been smuggled into the US with his parents, hidden under a false floor in a van, only to end up in a car crash ten miles north of the border. He was found lying unharmed amid the twisted metal, crammed between the bodies of his dead parents.

That story always had the girls batting their pity-filled eyes at him.

Morons. They never bothered to see who Mateo really was.

Maybe Grady would always know him better than any woman.

When Mateo said nothing more about the book he'd read, Grady didn't push him on it. When he wanted to talk, he'd talk.

The silence stretched on for so long Grady practically jumped in his seat when Mateo finally spoke again.

"It said introverts usually prefer a small number of close friends over lots of casual ones." There was something very damaged and hurt and vulnerable about the way he sounded right then. Even in the low light of the moon, the look on his face matched the sound of his voice. "Most of their relationships can get pretty intense." He drank a long swallow of beer. Then another until the bottle was empty. He tossed it over his shoulder into the boat. "Who needs her?"

"Exactly." It wasn't like he'd been seeing her that long anyway. Grady handed him another beer.

Mateo didn't say anything else for a while, just stared off into the dark, impenetrable water once again. When that beer was almost gone, he said, "You know that thing we've been doing after your history class?"

Shit.

With that one question, he was violating their unspoken agreement not to talk about it—about what they did every Monday, Wednesday, and Friday when Grady got back to their dorm room.

So far those afternoons had been the best sexual experience of Grady's life, and all he did was spend those few minutes touching only himself.

With forced nonchalance he said, "Yeah."

"Was I cheating on her?"

"No fucking way! We were just beating off at the same time. It's not like we were doing it to each other. We weren't even on the same side of the damn room."

Mateo nodded, downed another long swallow.

Of course, it hadn't just been beating off, and they both knew it. The way they'd watched each other, focused on the other man's dick as he worked it over. They had matched their rhythms so it was exactly like they were doing it to each other. And neither one would look away until the other's pulse of cum shot out as he came.

For Grady it had all driven his arousal higher, made him come harder than anything else.

To his relief, they didn't say anything more on the subject. They kept on twisting open beers until they were both drunk, cursing at the fish who sporadically breached the surface of the water, laughing at how every rustle of brush and crack of a twig from the acres of wooded land surrounding the lake had them jumping out of their seats.

They finished off the last of the beers a few hours later, and then Mateo passed out on his side on the canoe floor. Too tired and drunk himself, Grady ungracefully ducked under the thwart that stretched across the canoe's middle and squeezed in beside him. Sometime in the night Grady's arm became a pillow, protecting Mateo's head from that hard, wet floor.

When they awoke, the lake was covered in fog, the sunrise a brilliant orange burning through the mist. The sorrowful call of a mourning dove was punctuating the quiet stillness.

Without a word they got up and arranged themselves on the seats.

As if they had to summon the energy to move, they sat there holding on to the oars, facing each other, both staring off into the separating fog, watching a pair of swans take flight and breeze across the surface of the water.

"Thanks," Mateo said in a low whisper.

"No problem."

He nodded, then looked Grady's way.

Grady added, "I always got your back."

* * * *

Two hours later Grady was balancing a bag of groceries on his hip as he opened the door to the guest cottage. He got one step in and froze.

Mateo was lying naked on the lone bed—where Grady usually slept—one hand tucked behind his head, the other gripping his cock.

Just the way Grady had watched him jerk off so many times in their dorm room, watched that slick hand running along the length of his shaft, listened to his breathing pick up speed, the groans he'd let out right before he came.

Mateo didn't scramble to cover himself, and Grady didn't look away. He stepped farther inside and swung the door closed behind him. He dropped the grocery bag on the kitchen table as he passed by and went to the couch—where Mateo usually slept.

Mateo hadn't taken his eyes off Grady, and he hadn't let go of his dick.

Neither of them said a word as Grady sat on the couch and reached to undo his jeans. Mateo started stroking again, and

Grady slipped a hand inside his underwear, frantically trying to catch up. It wasn't going to take long. Not with the way Mateo was watching his hand move underneath the fabric.

Then Mateo turned away. He reached for his bag that was sitting on the nightstand. He tossed Grady a bottle of lubricant—the girlie shit with some sort of imitation cherry flavoring. Grady squirted a glob on his palm and fished out his cock. He worked it over, quickly getting it to a state of desperation. He hadn't gone at it with such vigor in a long while.

Of course, he had never gone this long without sex. The last serious thing he'd had going with a girl had ended six months earlier, and since then he hadn't felt inclined to hook up with anyone.

Not when he had something this good.

Was he really saying that jerking off was better than sliding his dick into a wet, hot pussy?

Right now? *Hell yeah.*

They sat there fixated on each other, the sound of their slick strokes filling the room.

Mateo moaned, threw his head back on the pillow. He dropped his free hand to the sheet beside him and gripped it in his fist. "Grady!" Cum spurted out of him and landed on his abs, his hips slamming up again and again with his release.

That had Grady working himself faster.

"Your turn," Mateo said around a sigh, gaze locked on the steady tugging action of Grady's hand.

That did it. Grady groaned and came, his body quivering, and through it all he never looked away from Mateo—who was still watching him in return.

In all the times they'd been doing this, Mateo had never said his name. He'd never said anything.

Grady was still wringing the cum from his cock when Mateo swung his legs off the side of the bed, facing the opposite wall. He stood and slipped on his jeans, his broad shoulders and biceps flexing.

How had he so casually gotten up and gotten dressed like that? While Grady was still gasping for breath?

Only then did Grady realize how he'd been watching Mateo's every move, taking in the sight of him—his naked body, his strong frame and hard muscles—in a way that scared the shit out of him.

He wanted him.

He wanted to touch his dick, have Mateo touch him in return.

He wanted to grab that ass he'd just been staring at.

He wanted Mateo to...

To fuck him.

"Shit!" Grady dropped his head to the couch behind him, trying not to panic, trying to figure out when things with his best friend had changed that much, and what the hell he was going to say to him.

Fuck that. He wasn't saying anything.

Because this was crazy. He was straight. Snatch-eating, pussy-fucking, tit-licking *straight*.

So they'd done some jerking off together? Big deal.

He was *not*—

He couldn't even think the word.

There was just something about Mateo, something about watching him pleasure himself that got Grady hot and bothered. It fed a primal instinct in him that no amount of fucking girls had done for him.

Jerking off together was bound to mix thoughts of Mateo and sex together in his mind. He was just horny and stressed about finals coming up and feeling weird about no longer living with Mateo in a few weeks.

That was it. That was all it was.

He sensed Mateo's presence before he felt his touch. Mateo placed a hand on each of Grady's knees and knelt on the floor before him.

The look on his face was a new one. Fear?

"I can't lose you, our friendship... That would be..." He shook his head. "Impossible."

What the hell?

"You're not gonna lose me."

Mateo's expression grew more pronounced—more unsure

than Grady had ever seen him. He always had a confidence about him that went well with his quiet, stoic persona. Most people took all that to mean he was a tough guy who never let himself feel anything. When really, he had felt things so deeply he'd learned to keep himself at bay from almost everyone and everything to avoid the pain.

Grady knew what Mateo was saying. Grady was his family. So were his siblings and his parents, his aunts and uncles, his cousins. They were the only real family Mateo had ever known.

But Mateo was overthinking this.

"You're not gonna lose me," Grady repeated.

Mateo reached up and grabbed him by the back of the neck. He licked his lips and watched Grady's. He leaned in. Grady could feel Mateo's warm breath graze the surface of his lips, like a caress.

Was he going to—

No. He wouldn't. Would he?

Then Mateo stopped. He pulled back.

Without another moment's hesitation, he stood and went across the room to the kitchen area. He rinsed his hands in the sink. Then, with fierce concentration, he started unloading the groceries, checking out each item like he had to read the entire ingredient list before he could put it away.

"What—" Grady started, then stopped, not sure what the hell he was going to say, or what he wanted to say.

Mateo looked his way, one dark eyebrow raised. "Something wrong?"

Grady swallowed but couldn't find his voice.

When he didn't say more, Mateo asked, "What?"

Shaking his head, Grady croaked out, "Nothing." He grabbed the tissues from the end table, cleaned up, and got off the couch. He swiped one of the new boxes of cereal off the kitchen table and went for a bowl in the cupboard. He didn't pour the cereal, though. He tried to keep his back to Mateo, but he couldn't even do that. He was so flabbergasted he just turned around and stood there with his arms folded across his chest, staring at Mateo's profile while Mateo kept casually removing items from the bag one at a time.

Grady wanted to grab hold of the package of chocolate-chip cookies and fling it out the damn window.

Mateo set the cookies down and went on with the unloading. Finally he reached the end of the groceries but kept his focus on the last item—a can of flaming red-hot barbecue chips.

That was when it hit Grady.

"You're freaked out."

"No!" Mateo slammed the can of chips onto the table, smashing the package of cookies in the process. "I'm not."

"You are." Grady seized him by the arm and spun him around. "Teo, it doesn't have to mean anything. So we like jerking off together? It doesn't mean we're— It doesn't mean anything."

Mateo snorted out a bitter laugh and shook his head. "It means everything."

What the hell was he implying by that? Grady couldn't bring himself to ask.

Mateo's entire body seemed to relax; his expression softened like he'd made his mind up about something and was completely comfortable with the decision. "What if I want something more than what we've been doing?" His gaze narrowed in on Grady again. "What if I think you do too?"

Suddenly Grady couldn't swallow. Breathing normally was also getting pretty tricky.

Because he did want it.

God, how he wanted it.

Did that mean—

"Yeah," Mateo said. "And that's why I'm freaked."

"What—" Grady was finding it difficult to focus. He wasn't sure what Mateo was trying to say. The thought of this ending—of not getting the last few weeks of school doing what they'd been doing together—was more than a little disappointing. He just knew he'd have said or done almost anything to get him to stop talking, to get him back on the bed with his cock out again.

Mateo crossed the small space separating them and stopped before him. He had that nervous, almost scared look in his eyes again.

Grady spoke first. "It doesn't mean dick, okay?"

Mateo laughed at that.

Yeah, poor choice of words. He tried again. "And no matter what, we're good. Nothing changes that. Got it?"

Mateo met his stare. He must've seen something in Grady's expression as well, something that told him Grady wanted this the same way he did, that Grady would give just about anything to repeat what they'd done a moment ago.

"Okay." Mateo moved in closer. His mouth was turned up at the corners in a teasing smirk Grady had seen from him a lot over the years. "Is it locked? Knowing your family, they'd just barge right in."

"What?"

He took another step, and his voice dropped lower. "Is the door locked?"

"Yeah." Grady's brain was having a hard time keeping up with him. Mateo was so close to him now, their bodies almost touching, Mateo's mouth mere inches from Grady's own. So close that when Mateo spoke, Grady could feel that warm breath on his lips again.

"Good." Mateo shifted on his feet, bringing them even closer. Their jean-covered thighs brushed one against the other.

What the hell were they doing?

Mateo bit his bottom lip and slowly released it. Then in a quick move, he cupped the back of Grady's neck and leaned in. Just like on the couch. Only this time he didn't stop.

The first press of his mouth to Grady's was a soft touch that grew more urgent, more desperate with every second. He turned them and backed Grady out of the kitchen area and up against the closed door of the guesthouse, bringing his full weight into him, rocking against him, holding Grady's head in his strong hands.

A minute into that kiss, and Grady's body was ready to explode with a release he never thought could come from just one kiss.

Then their tongues connected.

An electric current shot through him. He grabbed on to Mateo in return, holding him by the hips, forcing Mateo to move against him again, to brush that lean, hard body against his cock over and over. He couldn't help but notice how very strong and masculine Mateo felt in his hands—and how fucking good that felt.

The door rattled behind them with their movements. There was nothing slow or easy about the kiss, about the way they rocked against each other.

A primal need had erupted inside Grady, leaving him unable—and unwilling—to stop the desire blazing through him.

"Teo," he said around a moan as Mateo kissed a path down his neck. "What are we doing?"

"Christ, Grady. I don't know, but I don't want it to stop."

Fucking hell, he didn't want it to stop either.

He wanted more, everything he had pretended he wasn't picturing during their past few jerk-off sessions.

Mateo pulled back. He stared at Grady's lips again, licked his own. "Fuck." He shook his head as if to clear his thoughts. Or maybe not. He propped a hand against the door beside Grady and leaned in once more.

Their mouths met again, and that was it. Grady gave himself over to the moment—over to Mateo.

Mateo's lips slid to his earlobe, and he whispered, "I wanna suck your dick."

Grady whimpered. He couldn't keep the reaction at bay if he'd wanted to.

Mateo ran those lips down along the sensitive skin of his neck again, nipping and licking as he went, sweeping his hands up under Grady's T-shirt, over the flesh of his bare chest. "I wanna fuck you all goddamn night."

Grady forced Mateo's head up so they were face-to-face. "Shut up and kiss me again."

Only he didn't really want him to shut up. He wanted to hear every word. He wanted exactly what Mateo was describing.

He wanted it all. Every fucking thing.

Chapter One

Grady could not stop staring at the guy wearing the black leather boots and a rainbow swimsuit that covered about as much as a jockstrap. No pants, no shirt, just skin and more skin. With round, taut ass cheeks that flexed with every step, he was a big guy, more muscular than Grady. And Grady wasn't a small man.

Rainbow Jockstrap Guy also sported black cuffs around each wrist like he was just waiting for another guy to tie him down and do all sorts of delicious things to him.

Grady forced himself to look somewhere else—anywhere else.

A drag queen in high heels sauntered past in skintight stretch pants that showcased a firmly packed cock and balls hidden under the pink, sequined fabric. Grady tried not to stare. It was just all so damn...*new* for him. Even during his college years, he hadn't done anything like checking out a pride parade—not that he would've considered something like that back then.

The crowd around him cheered at the next parade float that passed by, decked out in all white carnations and roses with gay and lesbian couples on board in full wedding apparel. On the side of the float was painted *Happy Pride from your friends at West Clinton Community Church.*

This was not what he'd expected when he'd made the decision that morning to check out the late-summer pride events.

He'd just been hoping to find out where guys usually went to hook up. And if he got very lucky, find an interested, nameless guy at the parade so he could test out the waters, see if he could really follow through on what he'd been feeling. He'd only ever tried with one guy before, and that had ended badly.

Of course, that had been all his fault.

Since then he'd spent a lot of time contemplating just how much he'd fucked it up.

But not today.

Today was about something else.

Sex. Plain and simple.

Although could sex with a guy ever be simple?

Maybe not for someone like him who'd spent six years living a lie.

Did that matter anymore?

He was ready now. He wanted to get fucked by a man. He wanted some guy's large hands all over him. He wanted to be touched and stroked and kissed.

Yeah, he even wanted that basic pressing together of two mouths, two tongues, hands exploring as lips did the same.

He glanced across the street again as soon as the church float was by, hoping to catch another look at the big guy in the swimsuit. Apparently twinks weren't going to be his thing.

That was when he saw him.

Not Rainbow Jockstrap Guy.

Mateo Alvarez.

The best friend he'd ever had.

And the only guy who'd ever touched his dick. The only one who'd ever kissed him.

Fucking hell, he'd never been kissed like that.

Still hadn't.

That moment was one of the reasons he now found himself standing along the parade route, finally accepting he was gay. Six years of jerking off to one memory was pretty telling. He'd also been dreaming of so many things he wanted to do to Mateo—and vice versa—things they never had a chance to explore.

And now here he was.

Grady stared at him across the slew of bears on bikes who were cruising down the parade route. Mateo wore low-riding jeans and a snug black tank top. He definitely hadn't let himself go since their college days. At six-two he was only an inch taller than Grady, and there was no doubt he would still keep up with Grady in the weight room. He had a dusting of dark facial hair that was sexy as hell. Grady wasn't sure he'd ever seen him skip shaving like that, not when he was out in public. His black hair was a little longer than when Grady had last seen him at their graduation.

Mateo had his arms folded across his chest, hands gripping the curves of his biceps, a slight scowl on his face as he ignored the parade and scanned the crowd in every direction. Then he got a look across the street. At Grady.

Mateo stopped. Stared. His eyes widened; his lips parted.

"Mateo!" Grady shouted over the rumble of the bikes between them.

That surprised look was gone. Pain descended over his features, followed by anger. His eyes narrowed.

Yeah, he recognized him.

Then in a flash he turned his back on Grady and took off.

For a second or two Grady just stood there, shocked at actually seeing the guy from every one of his fantasies.

Then he got moving. No way was Mateo going anywhere until they talked. Until Grady had a chance to apologize. To say what he should've been man enough to say that weekend at the lake—the last weekend they'd spent together.

Grady raced out onto the street, between the lines of bikes, to the sidewalk on the other side. It didn't take long, and he had Mateo in his sights again. Mateo was moving at a quick clip down a side street away from the parade. He rounded the corner of the next building, and Grady sprinted after him.

Only, when he turned the corner, the alley was empty. Mateo was gone.

"Fuck!"

Why the hell hadn't he moved faster?

And why had Mateo taken off like that?

Screw that. He knew why.

Halfway down the alley, a chain-link fence blocked the way. There was only one door leading to the building on the right. Nothing on the left. Grady checked the door. Locked. Had

Mateo gone in there and locked the door behind him? Or had he scaled the fence? He wasn't walking or running down the alley. Maybe he hadn't rounded that corner at all.

Or maybe he'd been wicked fast, determined to lose Grady. Which was pretty telling, and probably a sign Grady should let this—and him—go.

He couldn't.

He went back out onto the street. Mateo was nowhere in the crowd.

Grady searched, pushed past people on one side of the street, then the other. He went back to the parade and scanned the crowd there. For two hours he did the same thing in the courtyard where the vendor booths were on display, but there was no sign of him. Eventually, reluctantly, he gave in and made his way to his truck.

He had no reason to stay, no reason to look for anyone else.

Fuck sex with some nameless stranger. There was only one man he wanted.

One man he had never gotten over.

Now that he'd seen him again, he knew... He *had* to find Mateo.

It was more than the sexual fantasies. Every memory, every touch, every feeling he'd had for him came rushing back when those dark eyes looked his way.

* * * *

With a ding, Grady's phone signaled a new e-mail. Another reply to his Facebook post. This one from a cousin on his mom's side of the family.

What the hell? You're a fag? I do not want to know this.

Grady sighed and sank back in the chair where he sat at the kitchen table. It had been two weeks since he'd posted a message on his Facebook page, and another one on the public page for the West Clinton Pride Parade, explaining that he was trying to locate Mateo—and why. Two weeks and people were still seeing the posts, still commenting on them.

He had wanted to go talk to his family—mostly his brothers and sisters—in person, but he'd been beyond nervous about it and had decided to go the more passive Facebook route. Plus, he didn't want to wait any longer to post the message about Mateo. Six years had been long enough. Time to make a grand gesture that Mateo wouldn't miss—so long as someone actually told him about it, which seemed less and less likely with each passing day.

Grady had gotten calls and e-mails from a number of family and friends. Most people were cool about it. Some even wanted to set him up with gay guys they knew. A few assholes had said they were praying for him, and then they immediately unfriended him, but they were by far the minority.

His baby sister had stopped by to cuss him out for not calling her. He'd opened the door, and she'd lunged at him, wrapping her arms around him in a tight embrace. *"Oh my God. You and Mateo! Why didn't you say something?"*

Okay, so maybe a message in his Facebook news feed was not the best way to come out to his family. At least he'd decided to go see his parents first so he could tell them in person.

His mom had cried for two hours, puttering around the house, dusting knickknacks that had no dust, mumbling about grandchildren and how she'd had no idea, before she'd hugged him and said, *"Gay or straight, it doesn't matter. We love you."* Although apparently she'd first needed to grieve for the straight son she'd thought he'd been all his life.

His dad was a little more stoic about the whole thing—even throughout the two hours of his wife's crying. After she'd finished, he'd finally spoken with a slight smile on his lips, shaking his head. "I always wondered about the two of you."

About him and Mateo?

Had his dad been the only one?

People thinking that exact thing about them had been a big part of why Grady had run from Mateo after that weekend they'd spent together at the lake.

How much of an asshole did that make him?

Because now that everyone knew, his family, his friends… Almost none of it had been the reaction he'd feared six years ago—at least not from the people who mattered—which had him feeling like an even bigger asshole.

He had to find Mateo.

Before posting the messages on Facebook, he'd spent a week scouring the Internet looking for him—for a phone number, a physical address, an e-mail, a Facebook account, anything. All he'd come up with was an old university address—his own old address too since there hadn't been a day during school when they didn't live together.

Well, all except for those last few weeks leading up to graduation.

He had also called and e-mailed every mutual friend he could think of and had gone to see Mateo's uncle. No one knew where Mateo lived or worked. All his uncle had said was that he hadn't seen him in more than three years, and then he'd slammed the door in Grady's face.

The only option Grady could come up with was to try to find someone on Facebook who'd been at the parade and who knew Mateo. There had to be a reason he'd gone there.

Grady's phone dinged with another new message.

From someone he didn't know this time.

Don't know Mateo, but have you tried posting in the personals on craigslist? Lots of gay guys read those.

Grady sat up straight and reread the message. He grinned—a ridiculously wide smile—as a surge of adrenaline shot through him.

He fumbled with his phone, sent a hurried thank-you to the man who'd replied to his post, and got out his computer. He'd been on craigslist before, but he'd never gone looking in the personals section, let alone the *Men Seeking Men* ads.

Browsing the local site, he found a category titled *Missed Connections*. He clicked on the link and scanned the posts. The sheer number of married men looking for other married men they'd spotted while they were out somewhere with their wives was astounding. As were the number of random, nameless hookups trying to find each other again. Their blatant descriptions of what they'd done together—and what they wanted to do next—captivated him. He kept reading, shifting in his seat as he clicked on link after link.

He was getting hard just going through the posts. Why

hadn't he checked out these listings before now? He might've had the nerve to meet up with someone years ago.

Of course, with the back-to-back women he'd been seeing—and the two he'd married—that would've made him a cheater. No matter how either of his marriages had ended, he wouldn't have wanted to hurt them like that, or any of the women he'd been seeing.

Answering an ad also might have meant he would've had sex with a guy who wasn't Mateo.

He was surprised by how much he liked the idea that Mateo would be the first one. The only one?

That was if he ever saw him again.

If he ever got him in his bed again.

He started a new *Missing Connections* post and began typing.

OLD COLLEGE ROOMMATE SPOTTED AT PRIDE PARADE

Mateo, I've been looking everywhere for you. I need to see you, need to talk to you. Have not stopped thinking about you or that last weekend we spent together. I wanted you to fuck me so bad, and I've never regretted anything more than not telling you that, than not having sex with you that weekend. You're the only guy I've ever been with, and now I know you're the only guy I want. I've spent the past six years thinking about you, missing everything about you. I need to see you.

Then he listed the one thing he wanted Mateo to do to him the most, the one fantasy that got him hard and got him off faster than anything else.

He stopped typing. He closed his eyes and let the memories of that last weekend with Mateo wash over him. Every touch, every kiss, the way Mateo's hands felt on him, the way his lips and body felt pressed against his own as they thrust and rocked and stroked and kissed.

He opened his eyes and stared across the room to the bed on the other side of the guesthouse. He'd been living there at the lake for the past six months, lying there in that bed, picturing everything they'd done, and imagining everything they'd never gotten a chance to do.

Now he thought back on how that day had ended, and how very differently the next morning could've gone if he'd been stronger, braver. More like Mateo.

He *had* to see him again.

He returned to the craigslist message on his computer and hit Submit.

* * * *

The doorbell rang, and then the knocking started.

"Grady Flynn, open this fucking door!"

Grady didn't move from where he sat on the couch staring at the muted TV. He'd put on a movie an hour ago but had gotten bored halfway through and turned off the sound, letting the glow from the screen keep him company in the dark room.

He wasn't in the mood to talk to anyone. Let alone his baby brother.

Although he was surprised Riley had driven out to the lake. He rarely came anymore, even though he now worked in the area.

"Open up, Grady. I know you're in there. Your truck's outside, and I saw you through the damn window."

Grady gave in and went to the door. Riley stood on the other side wearing his deputy sheriff's uniform, looking pissed off and not afraid to express it.

Why couldn't Grady's family ever hold in their feelings?

Riley kept on glaring at him. It was like looking in a mirror. Everyone always said they could pass as twins.

"So...you're a goddamn homo?"

"Shut the fuck up." Grady tried to slam the door in his face.

Riley wasn't having any of that. He had his shoe jammed in the way. "Why didn't you tell me you're a fag?" He gave a good shove to the door. He had gotten stronger since he'd slapped on the badge.

Grady gave up, crossed the room, and dropped onto the couch. "Don't say it like that."

"What the hell am I supposed to say?" Riley flipped on the overhead light, shocking Grady with its harsh glare.

It took his eyes a moment to adjust. Apparently he'd been sitting for too long in the dark, trying to figure out his next move.

Riley stood before him, his thumbs hooked in his gun belt. "You've slept with more women than I've known in my entire life."

"So what?"

Grady's phone went off again. Another new e-mail message. He clicked to open it.

Where are you? Tell me, and I'm on my way.

At those words his heartbeat kicked up a notch.

Until he read the rest. *I'll fuck that virgin cumhole of yours.*

Definitely not Mateo.

The use of *cumhole* alone told him that. Most of the replies had been that way. Before he'd posted the message, he had assumed he wouldn't know for sure if any of them were from Mateo until he talked to him on the phone and heard him say his name.

He could still remember the last time he'd heard it.

Grady had been about to walk out the door of their dorm room, all his shit packed and in his truck. In a cracked, strained voice, Mateo had said, *"Don't go."* Then he'd whispered, *"Grady, please don't go."*

And Grady had said nothing in return.

He ignored the lingering glare from his brother and deleted the e-mail. That was the forty-ninth one that day. All from guys wanting to fuck his *virgin* ass. He wasn't sorry he'd posted the ad. He was just sorry he got so damn excited with every new e-mail, hoping, believing any one of them would be Mateo.

His phone signaled another message. Another guy looking to fuck him.

"What the hell is up with your phone?" Riley asked, still standing over him.

"Nothing."

"Bullshit. I saw that look on your face when you read that last one. Tell me what's going on."

His phone rang this time. He checked the display. Not a number he recognized.

He fumbled to answer the call. "Hello."

"Take that ad off craigslist."

That voice…

"Mateo." All that time he'd been waiting to talk to him, and all he could come up with to say was his name? Grady shifted the phone to his other ear, farther away from his brother. "I need to see you," he managed to add.

"No." Mateo spat out the word in a curt tone that said it wasn't up for discussion. "Take the stupid ad down. You practically called yourself a virgin. You're going to be harassed by guys."

Yeah, he was.

He wasn't sure how Mateo had gotten his number, but if he'd seen the ad and that was what got him to track Grady down, it was worth it. "It doesn't matter. I had to find you."

Silence on the other end. Then finally, "I don't want to see you. Just let this go, and take that ad down."

Mateo had spoken in a less angry tone, and the hint of concern in his voice canceled out any worry that Grady might've made the wrong decision in looking for him.

"If you don't want to see me, then why did you call?"

Again Mateo said nothing.

Riley was intently staring down at Grady on the couch. The look of betrayal had vanished, and he was watching him with curiosity.

Grady got up and crossed the room to the kitchen area. With the open layout of the guesthouse, that move only offered a semblance of privacy. Riley had to be hearing everything. Grady didn't care. Not now.

He rested his head against the refrigerator and spoke into the phone. "Why can't you just talk to me?"

A long, grave sigh came over the line. "I just…"

Grady waited for him to finish.

Mateo didn't. The line went dead.

Grady hit the button to return the call. No answer. No voice mail. Nothing. He hung up and tried again. Same thing. Again. The same.

He kept his forehead pressed to the freezer door, the phone clutched in his fist. He remained perfectly still like maybe Mateo would call back if he didn't move. Riley's voice from behind him broke the silence.

"Why didn't you come to me? I could've helped you find him."

Was he serious? Hadn't he heard himself when he'd gotten there a few minutes ago?

Grady spun to face him. He must've managed a ticked-off enough expression.

Riley said, "I was just pissed you didn't tell me. I had to read that my brother's a queer on *Facebook*. I felt like an idiot."

"Yeah." Grady's frustration eased some. He went back to sit on the couch. "That was a shitty thing to do."

His brother followed. "Fuck yeah, it was." He returned to standing before the couch, arms folded over his chest. "I felt like I was the last person in the whole damn world to know. You never once let on."

Grady shrugged. "I'm just now getting to where I can accept this about myself."

"So you and Mateo weren't…" He made a fucking gesture with his hips. "All that time back then?"

"Jeez. No."

"Oh." He moved to sit beside him, eyebrows raised. "Really?"

"Just…" Grady sighed. "Just once, but we didn't fuck."

Riley studied him with obvious skepticism. "Once?"

"Yes! One time." One fucking incredible time.

Riley held up his hands in surrender. "All right." They sat in the quiet for a minute. Then he asked, "That was him on the phone?"

"Yeah."

"He won't see you?"

"No."

"And you still don't know where he's living?"

"Nope."

Riley searched his face again. Grady felt like a suspect Riley was about to press for more information.

Which he did. "Why do you want to talk to him so bad?"

"I want to apologize and explain why I left, why I hurt him."

"You don't think he knows? You were a chickenshit, right?"

"Fuck you!" Grady surged off the couch. "You don't get it. You've never had to tell anyone—"

"That I like dick? Hey, if I was into it, I wouldn't give a shit what anyone said."

Grady gave him a long stare, then dropped back to the couch beside him. "You're an idiot."

Riley made a dismissive gesture in the air. "I get it. Easy for me to say. It's not six years ago. I'm not a star hockey player. And I'm not a cocksucker. What do I know, right?"

When Grady didn't respond, Riley focused on the picture window across the room that looked out over the lake, a thoughtful expression on his face. Eventually he added, "If I *were* a cocksucker, I bet I'd be real damn good at it. I got skills with the snatch."

Grady rolled his eyes. "If you had that much skill, you wouldn't have a new girlfriend every month."

"Hey." Riley slapped Grady's thigh with the back of his hand like he'd just thought of something. "You wanna give my new girl some tips? Man, she has no idea what she's doing down there, and we both know it. Now she'll barely put her lips below my waist." He looked dead serious.

"Shut up."

"I'm not shitting you, man. She needs some major pointers. I could bring her by tonight. I mean, isn't that supposed to be one of the advantages of having a gay brother?"

"I'm not giving lectures to every girl you want to blow you."

But Grady knew his brother. He wasn't going to let this go.

"Besides…"

"What?" Riley asked.

"She's got more experience than I do."

He laughed at that, then bolted upright. "Wait! You've never sucked a guy off?"

He took Grady's silence as the affirmation it was. He threw his arms up in the air. "How in the hell did I get all the brains in this family? What kind of asshole tells his parents he's gay, announces it on Facebook for everyone to see, and he doesn't even know if he likes to suck dick?" He laughed again, then suddenly grew thoughtful, studying Grady. "You ever take it up the ass?"

"Shut. Up."

"Oh man." He fell back against the couch, laughing like he'd never met someone so ridiculous.

"I *had* to post that message. I had to find him." Grady knew he sounded more defensive than he'd meant to. Leaving the message on Facebook had been about more than just finding Mateo. "He was at the pride parade."

"So? What does that matter?"

Grady gestured with his arm. "He's obviously out. Probably has been for years. If I have any chance with him, he has to know I'm ready this time. That I won't freak out and take off again. I figured showing him I was out too couldn't hurt."

Riley rubbed his jaw and considered Grady for another minute. The next word out of his mouth was spoken more seriously than anything he'd said since he'd arrived. "Okay." Then he stood and went to sit at the kitchen table. He tugged Grady's laptop toward him and opened the lid. "People just don't disappear. Give me that number he called from. I'll see if I can track down an address."

Grady got up and handed him his phone. "Don't do anything you'll get in trouble for."

Riley glared at him in disbelief, then said, "Fine. I won't use official channels. There are public websites that list current and former addresses."

"I tried that. All I got was an address from back in school."

"I might know of sites you don't. He had to have paid bills at some point. A credit card, phone, electric, something."

Riley spent the next half hour searching online while Grady sat opposite him and tried not to show his rising anxiety.

Finally Riley looked up from the computer. "The phone number's a dead end. He doesn't have a valid driver's license or current address listed anywhere. All I can find is this one." He wrote the address down and handed Grady the piece of paper. "It's listed as a former address. It doesn't say from how long ago. If he's not still there, maybe you can see if anyone there knows him, or knows where he moved to."

The address was in a part of West Clinton Grady was unfamiliar with, where no one he knew would hang out, let alone live.

"He must not want to be found," Riley added. He wouldn't meet Grady's gaze.

"What aren't you telling me?"

He didn't respond.

"Riley."

"I didn't exactly use *unofficial* channels. Which means..." Riley looked Grady's way, his expression somber. "It takes a lot of effort to disappear the way he has."

Effort?

What was Mateo hiding from?

Grady stared at the address in his hand. "What do I do now? He wouldn't talk to me."

Riley was quiet for another moment. Then he reached for his belt. He threw Grady a sly smile and held up a pair of handcuffs. "Make him listen."

Chapter Two

The restaurant was a little Italian joint housed in a narrow brick building, nestled between a sports bar and one of those instant-payday-loan places. The restaurant's front door, and the sign hanging overhead, were so unobtrusive if you weren't looking for the place, you'd pass right on by and not even notice.

Grady walked by on purpose and turned into the first alley he came to, then went around to the back of the building. The steps leading to the second-floor apartment were tucked off to the side. Again, nothing noticeable unless someone was looking specifically for them.

He climbed the rickety wooden staircase and knocked on the apartment door. He waited, but when there was no answer to a second knock, he headed back down to the restaurant. Someone there might know Mateo or at least know if he still lived in the apartment above.

The lighting inside the restaurant was dim. All the tables and booths had seating for no more than four people, with clusters of lit votive candles as the centerpieces, giving the place a cozy, intimate feel.

The early dinner crowd had cleared out, which made it easier to spot the dark-haired man balancing a tray of four coffee mugs. He walked toward a booth in the back, moving with a confident, low-key stride that matched the man Grady had known six years ago. He hadn't shaved again, and the facial hair gave him the look of someone very different from that same man. Like someone who was hiding something, someone who was dangerous.

Grady asked the hostess for a table up front, hoping Mateo's section didn't extend that far. What he had planned could not take place in a public restaurant.

Following the hostess to his seat, he couldn't take his eyes off Mateo. In black pants and matching black dress shirt and tie, he was wearing more fabric than three weeks ago at the parade, but somehow he looked even sexier.

He had stopped at another table and was smiling at the couple in the booth. They were sitting close on the same side, holding hands, their heads together as they laughed over a shared joke.

That pleasant grin, and the way Mateo kept the smile going as he talked to the couple and took their orders, was remarkably different from the expression worn by the cautious, nervous man he'd been at the parade—even before he'd spotted Grady across the sea of men on bikes.

He seemed relaxed, at ease in this space, less on guard.

As he left the couple's table and headed for a doorway leading to the kitchen, Grady sat taller, anxiety settling in his gut at the thought of Mateo turning in the order and walking out the back door.

He might never see him again.

A ridiculous reaction perhaps, but there it was.

Even if Mateo took off again, Grady was not giving up until he talked to him, until Mateo listened.

Hence his brother's spare set of handcuffs tucked in his back pocket.

Mateo exited the kitchen a few minutes later. Grady shifted sideways to hide behind a potted fern sitting on the ledge between booths.

That fern was his salvation for the next hour and a half as he ate a plate of rigatoni and every basket of breadsticks the waitress brought so he wouldn't be asked to leave.

Sometime later when Mateo handed off his tables to a coworker, Grady paid his bill. He made his way outside and down the alley. He stayed close enough to the back of the restaurant that he wouldn't miss Mateo's exit, but out of sight so no one saw him skulking about in the dark.

Five minutes later Mateo walked out the back door. He

didn't go up the stairs to the apartment above. He headed south, keeping close to the buildings in the darkened shadows. After three blocks, he stopped and climbed a flight of stairs beside the rear entrance to an adult video and bookstore. The stairs were more dilapidated than the ones at the apartment above the restaurant.

Grady followed as quietly as he could manage while making it up the creaking stairs before Mateo had the apartment door closed. At the top of the stairs he raced forward, shuffled Mateo inside, and kicked the door closed behind them.

"What the—" Mateo spun around, fists up, ready to strike.

Which he did.

Grady successfully dodged the punch. But another followed.

"Mateo!"

Then another punch. Grady had his arms in front of his face, deflecting the jabs.

"It's me. Grady."

Mateo stopped fighting but kept on guard. The confused stare, the panicked look on his face had Grady feeling like a jackass. Why the hell couldn't he have knocked on the damn door?

Because Mateo might not have opened it once he realized who the guy on the other side was. And Grady couldn't take a chance, not after finally finding him.

"What are you doing here?" Mateo spat the words out in a more pissed-off tone than Grady had ever heard from him. The anger didn't sound or look good on him. It just seemed wrong.

Completely wrong.

"I need to talk to you."

Mateo took a step back, his arms falling to his sides for a brief moment before they were tense again, folded across his chest. "Why?"

"To apologize. To explain why I left after…that weekend."

Mateo's hands squeezed tighter on his arms as if that was all that was keeping him from kicking Grady's ass out.

"To find out how you are," Grady added.

Mateo kept those arms folded, but his expression shifted slightly. To what? Grady wasn't sure.

So he kept talking, trying to forge a connection—any connection. "I made a mistake. A huge, gutless mistake."

Nothing but that tense stance, the hard stare.

"Come on. I was a stupid kid. Haven't you ever made a mistake?"

Mateo glared at him some more, said nothing. At least he wasn't trying to force Grady out of his home. Then finally he said, "You've got five minutes."

It was clear from his tone that five minutes wasn't going to cut it.

Grady scrambled to think of what to say. He should've had something substantial planned out. He'd just been so focused on finding him, on getting him alone.

"How have you been?" he asked.

Mateo didn't respond.

"How long have you been working at that restaurant?"

Nothing but another clench of his stubbled jaw.

Probably not Grady's best idea to start off with admitting he'd been following him and saw him leave the restaurant. Add that with the cuffs in his back pocket, and he was coming off like a stalker—even to himself.

"What happened to law school?" he asked. "The FBI?"

Mateo snorted out a short laugh, his gaze now locked on the scuffed, peeling vinyl floor between them.

At least it was a reaction. Something.

"Can we sit down?"

Mateo didn't make a move away from the door.

A low-wattage light—like a child's night-light—was on somewhere in the apartment, casting the place in an eerie, muted glow. The outlines of furniture were visible in the living room. A couch, a chair, but not much else. The windows were covered by black-out curtains that were taped along the sides to keep the light out. Or maybe it was to keep anyone else from seeing the light on inside.

On one wall, Grady could just barely see a large collection of papers tacked together. It looked like an enlarged city map. There were black marks all over the map, as well as notes and photographs tacked to the outer edges. It was too dark to make out any of the details, but it all said something to Grady.

Mateo was trying to find someone. Or he had them under surveillance. Or maybe it was all related to why *he* was so hard to find. Maybe he was actually in hiding.

"Why are you living here?"

He said nothing.

"What have you been doing all these years?"

Still nothing.

"Dammit, Teo, talk to me!"

Before that moment Grady had held back on using the nickname he'd always called Mateo.

Mateo met his stare, and for the first time since Grady had gotten there, he seemed to relax a touch—nothing anyone who couldn't read his reactions would pick up on.

But Grady had known him better than anyone.

"Thought you came here to explain," Mateo said.

Grady searched his face in the dim light, trying to see if he really could still read him. He wasn't so sure. Six years was a long time. Wasn't it? "I do want to explain."

"Too bad. Time's up. Now get the fuck out."

He might've left too. If he hadn't caught that look in Mateo's eyes, the way he was truly looking at him for the first time, practically drinking in the sight of him.

As if he could hear Grady's thoughts and wanted to show him how wrong he was, Mateo strode past him for the door and swung it open.

Grady stood his ground, his back to him. "No."

"Get out, Grady, or I'm calling the cops."

Hearing him say his name had him more determined than ever. He reached into his pocket and slapped one side of the cuffs on his own wrist, then turned and did the same to the arm Mateo had holding the door open.

"What the fuck?"

"I am not leaving here until we talk." He kicked the door shut.

Mateo jerked his cuffed arm, and then, as if that action confirmed that Grady had really cuffed them together, he lunged at him. Together they toppled over, Grady's back slamming into a small wooden table along one wall and knocking it over on the way down. The back of his head smacked the floor next, but that didn't stop Mateo.

He was on top of him. Like a feral beast, trying anything and everything to take Grady out. Slapping, punching, wrenching on the cuffs.

"Get this fucking thing off me!"

"Stop!" Grady shouted back and held up his free arm to defend himself. "You're gonna hurt yourself." He was going to hurt *both* of them.

Maybe it was the sound of Grady's voice, or maybe it was that Mateo realized he *was* hurting Grady, but in any case he stopped. He didn't move, though. He stayed on top of Grady, straddling him, his thighs tightly squeezing Grady's own, his chest heaving like he'd just been running for his life.

The press of Mateo's body over his was causing the same reaction Grady had every night since the parade, when he'd lain in his bed thinking of him, dreaming of Mateo's lips on his again, Mateo's mouth around his cock. That thought had him shifting beneath Mateo's weight, and his dick responded more with the friction of their bodies.

Mateo shifted too, moving up Grady's body, rubbing his ass over Grady's groin.

Grady wanted to believe it was an intentional move, but from the surprised look on Mateo's face at the involuntary groan that tore out of Grady's chest, he clearly hadn't meant to get him hard.

Mateo slid off him, and they separated.

Still cuffed together, they sat there side by side, Mateo's chest heaving again. Grady's did the same.

There was a knock on the door. A man called out. "Hey, man, you okay in there? The girls working the back room said they heard you breaking shit."

Mateo glanced Grady's way. He was watching him with that intense look of surprise and longing from earlier.

Another knock.

Mateo still didn't move. He said nothing.

Grady spoke low so only Mateo could hear. "Just give me this weekend. Just to talk. To catch up. One weekend, and if you want me to, I'll leave you alone after that."

From the other side of the door came, "Answer me, or I'm gonna bust the goddamn door down."

"You owe me," Grady added. He didn't want to play that card yet, but he couldn't think of another option. "For that night I stayed up with you and helped you study for that stats final. You passed and kept your scholarship that next semester. You told me you owed me. Anytime. Anywhere." He tilted his head forward until Mateo would look him in the eye. "Give me this one weekend."

Mateo hesitated for another minute. Then he got off the floor, and Grady scrambled up with him—the handcuffs gave him no other choice.

"Stay behind the door," Mateo ordered. He opened the door a crack, keeping their handcuffed arms out of sight. "Everything's fine," he told the guy who obviously worked in the porn shop downstairs.

"You sure?" the guy asked. "I don't want the cops showing up here in half an hour when whatever you got going on in there gets ugly."

"It won't. Promise. Listen, I need tomorrow off. I've got to take care of something."

"Are you shitting me? You're giving me one day's notice?"

Mateo didn't respond.

"Fine. But you're covering an extra day next week."

"Deal."

"You better not be bringing any trouble here."

"No trouble." Mateo leaned back and looked Grady's way. "I can handle it." He gave the man a nod and shut the door. He kept his hand flat against the surface, his back to Grady, more anger radiating off him.

"You work downstairs too?"

He didn't answer. He faced him and jerked the arm that was cuffed to Grady's. "Take these off me. Now!"

"You'll talk to me?"

For the first time Mateo looked at him as if he was seeing

an old friend—his best friend. There was still some anger there, but there was something else too.

And for a moment Grady feared he was being played. Had Mateo changed so much that he'd lie to him?

"I'll take them off as soon as we get where we're going."

Mateo stepped back until he was flat against the closed door, his cuffed arm out straight in front of him. His voice quivered a touch as he asked, "Going where?"

Even with the fact that Grady had sneaked up behind Mateo, shoved him into his apartment, brought handcuffs, and had used them on him, Mateo's reaction surprised him. He couldn't say he'd ever seen him looking so...

Scared.

"I'm not gonna hurt you."

"Where are we going?" His tone had turned hard again, demanding.

"Someplace we can be alone."

"Where?"

The plan that was ingenious earlier that day now seemed like a stupid, sentimental idea. Despite that, Grady forged ahead. He'd come this far, and Mateo had, at least seemingly, agreed to the weekend. "Where we spent that night."

Mateo glared at him. Then he scoffed as he looked away like it really was the stupidest, most sentimental idea he'd ever heard. But then his lips turned up at the corners. That relaxed, amused expression was probably not a reaction he'd meant to share, because he schooled it just as quickly.

Considering the frightened look he had sported earlier, how hard it had been to find him, as well as the way he was living in that dark, sparse hole of an apartment, there was no doubt in Grady's mind that something had happened to Mateo, and it wasn't good.

Why the hell had he listened to Riley about ambushing Mateo and using the cuffs in the first place? His brother had never had a real relationship in his entire adult life.

Grady uncuffed them, and Mateo snatched his hand back, covering his wrist with his other hand. But before he could move away, Grady told him, "You can trust me. Okay?"

Mateo skeptically studied him, and after a long pause, he nodded. The slightest movement of his head, but it was something.

Chapter Three

Mateo said nothing the entire drive, just stared out the passenger side of the truck like he never got out of the city anymore and didn't want to miss the last signs of summer still lingering in late September. With the window rolled down, the breeze hit his face as he watched the rows of corn and the ditches full of rose-colored milkweed whoosh by in the moonlight.

Or maybe Grady was fooling himself, and Mateo would stare at anything over looking at him again.

So much for the plan to get him to listen, to get Mateo to forgive him, to rekindle what they'd had. Grady's chances weren't looking good.

Then again, Mateo had agreed to come to the lake.

When they'd first gotten into the truck, he had sported that panicked look again. The same look a dog had when he was jammed into a crate, knowing he was headed to the vet for poking and prodding and painful shots.

Eventually Mateo seemed to relax. And when they pulled into the driveway leading to the Flynn family cottages, he gave up on staring out the side window and glanced around the property, at the fire pit on the beach, the boat launch, the faded wooden dock, and the expanse of red maple trees surrounding everything. Grady knew it all looked very much as it did six years ago.

Some things took longer to change than others.

The wistful look on Mateo's face matched how Grady felt right then.

Even though he'd been living at the lake for the past six

months, being there with Mateo brought back a rush of memories that had Grady frozen in his seat, gripping the steering wheel to keep from reaching out for him.

"Are we—" Mateo stopped abruptly.

When he didn't say more, Grady gestured to the smaller of the two houses. "We can stay in the guesthouse." Just like every time they'd been there before.

Like the last time.

Mateo gave a sharp nod and got out of the truck. He reached into the back for his bag. Then they stood side by side in front of the truck, Mateo glancing around again, gazing out at the water, at the path that led into the wooded area beyond the house, at the shed with the canoe tucked away inside.

Grady desperately wanted to ask if he was remembering the same moment in time—when they'd lugged out the canoe that last weekend they'd been there.

The next morning, when they'd been all set to paddle back to the house, Mateo had whispered one word. *"Thanks."*

A repeat of that same word brought Grady back to the present.

"For what?" he asked.

"Bringing me here instead of..." Mateo shrugged. "Anywhere else."

Grady nodded in understanding. Although he was certain he didn't know the real reason behind that whispered thanks.

Together they headed inside. Mateo set his bag on a chair by the door. Maybe he thought he might need to grab it in a hurry on his way out. He continued to take in the surroundings, like being there was some kind of strange mecca for him. Or maybe a salvation.

Same as the rest of the property, the one-room guesthouse wasn't all that different from when they'd stayed there during their college years. The same creaky hardwood floor, blue area rug covered in images of seashells, and wrought-iron headboard on the double bed in the corner of the room.

Mateo pointed to the couch.

Yeah, that was new. And about time too. "Mom and Dad finally threw out that old, nasty one."

It had been gold and gaudy with worn, stained fabric. Grady shuddered just thinking of all the times they'd plopped down on that couch in their soaking-wet, sand-ridden bathing suits that smelled of the fish they'd spent the afternoon swimming with.

When his parents had purchased the lake property, they had known it was an extravagance that would stretch their meager budget, but they'd wanted someplace for their extended family to gather. Aunts, uncles, cousins—hell, even the neighborhood kids who had no one but Grady's parents looking out for them—came there nearly every weekend during the summer.

Grady laughed, trying to ease the tension. "Remember when we hid all those frogs behind the cushions to scare my sisters?"

Mateo nodded, staring at the new couch. But seeing the old one?

"I swear we had a hundred of them jammed in there. After Mom stopped yelling, it took us all damn day to catch them and get them back outside."

Mateo chuckled then too. That laugh sounded good. Like Grady's childhood. Like afternoons playing video games and telling dirty jokes and chasing fireflies and roasting marshmallows over the fire pit.

But the laugh ended far too soon.

Mateo continued examining the rest of the space, and his expression shifted to something Grady couldn't read. Had he changed that much? Or had they lost that easy way they'd always understood each other without having to talk everything to death?

Mateo walked with stiff, unsure movements, like he'd just awoken from a long stint in a coma. Grady couldn't take his eyes off him—those broad shoulders and long legs, the way his black hair curled around the tops of his ears, the mole on the right side of his neck, the strong hands that ever so slightly clenched and unclenched as Mateo moved.

He eventually stopped before the framed photos of Grady's family and friends that sat on the low bookshelves under the picture window. He didn't say anything, just studied each one, then moved on to the next, until he reached the last one—a shot from the final hockey game of their senior year in college, their last win during the regular season. The entire team was in the picture, celebrating, arms around shoulders, hockey sticks raised in the air. Mateo and Grady were at the far end of the group, both smiling, Grady looking straight ahead at the camera. Mateo's gaze was locked on Grady, a lightness in his eyes, in his expression.

That look on his face was the reason Grady had hung on to the photo.

Saying nothing, Mateo turned his back on the pictures and once more surveyed the rest of the room.

Grady did the same thing, trying to envision how it all looked to Mateo—how different and yet the same.

When Mateo finally spoke, he asked, "You living here?"

"Yeah." Grady emptied his pockets and dropped his wallet, the handcuffs, and their key onto the nightstand beside the bed.

That disturbing unease was back on Mateo's face. The clench of his jaw was visible from across the room as he eyed the cuffs.

Grady opened the nightstand drawer and swiped the handcuffs inside. "I'm not gonna cuff you again. You promised me the weekend."

"Yeah, I did." Mateo met his stare. "I'm not the one who goes back on my word."

That hurt, but Grady deserved it.

He deserved worse.

He went back to Mateo's question. "She got the house in my last divorce. Been staying here since then."

"Last?"

"I've been married twice."

Mateo's brows rose at that.

"Neither one lasted very long."

Mateo regarded Grady for a few seconds longer, and then he turned his back to him once more, looking over the room again and every item in it with an intensity that had Grady feeling vulnerable, exposed.

But that was the point of bringing him here, wasn't it? To show him how different he was from that young, naive kid

Mateo had known. Yet how very much he was the same man too.

Mateo stopped again. This time in front of the hockey jersey hanging on the coat stand near the door.

Mateo's jersey.

Grady had taken it with him that last day he'd walked out of their dorm room.

Mateo faced him. He wore a shocked expression Grady couldn't quite interpret. Grady had hurt him—*again*—somehow, and he wasn't even sure how the hell he'd done it. Then Mateo asked, "Did they come here with you?"

"Who?"

"Your wives."

"No." Grady shrugged. "The timing was never right."

Mateo squinted at him, scrutinized him. It *was* hard to believe.

"They were real short marriages."

He nodded at that.

But what Grady had said wasn't the whole truth. His instincts told him to hold back on saying more, on letting any moment get too emotional, but that wasn't the point of bringing Mateo here. "I didn't want my memories of this place to change."

He had offered part of his truth and had hoped for a reaction, but there was nothing.

When Mateo stopped examining every inch of where Grady lived, he said, "And now you're..." He gestured up and down Grady's body but said nothing more.

"Gay?" Grady waited until Mateo nodded. "Guess I've always been gay. Just couldn't wrap my head around that before now."

Mateo huffed out a sound that seemed to be more one of annoyance and exasperation than amusement.

Grady sighed with his own frustration. He was saying all the wrong things. He moved toward Mateo. "I wanted to apologize for—"

Mateo shook his head. "Don't." He backed up a couple of uneven steps. "You want to spend the weekend here? Drink a few beers, shoot the shit, talk about our glory days playing hockey, tell me what you've been up to for the past six years of your life? Fine. But don't talk to me about those last three weeks of school. Don't talk to me about shit we can't change." He turned and stared out the picture window into the darkness of the lake, his body held tight, tension practically vibrating off him.

"Okay." Grady slowly, carefully moved in behind him. "But I am sorry, Teo. More than you'll ever know."

Mateo didn't move, just kept his gaze focused in the direction of the water lapping at the shore. Even with the moonlight, it was nearly impossible to see past the shoreline to the lake's surface beyond.

Grady tried another topic. "My mom said you called her for my phone number."

For a moment it didn't seem like Mateo was going to acknowledge that. Then he said a simple, "Yeah."

"I was trying to find you. Your uncle didn't know where you lived."

"I didn't want him to know."

"Why?"

Still facing the window, Mateo ran a hand through his dark hair, swiping back the strands coiled around his ear. The hair immediately settled back into place, curling over that ear again. Grady wanted to run his fingers through that black hair, lick that earlobe, bury his nose at Mateo's nape, and breathe in the scent of him. He couldn't stop staring at those wisps of hair, or at Mateo's bare neck, the defined muscles of his upper arms visible through the T-shirt sleeves, and the way the faded fabric of his jeans hugged the curve of his ass and clung to his thighs.

Mateo folded his arms across his chest and shrugged. "It doesn't matter."

Something told Grady he couldn't push. Not yet. He had to go slowly, let Mateo decide when to share more about his life, about why he'd been so hard to find.

But there was one thing Grady had been dying to know.

"Are you seeing anyone?"

Silence. Then Mateo faced him, eyes narrowed, scrutinizing

Grady again. There was even more anger aimed at him this time. "Not that it's any of your business, but no, I'm not."

That had the last of Grady's unease fading away. Bringing him here had been the right call.

He asked, "You ever been serious with anyone?"

Another pause. Mateo moved on to the kitchen area. He picked up a mug from the table and examined the Red Wings logo like he hadn't seen it in a long time.

Back in school they'd never missed a game on TV. Maybe he didn't watch hockey anymore.

Maybe he couldn't.

He returned the cup to the table. "I was once."

Hope that Mateo had meant him surged through Grady, but by that distant look on Mateo's face, it was clear he'd meant someone else.

A pang of jealousy hit Grady's gut, and for the first time, realization washed over him.

Mateo had fucked other guys—guys who were not him. He'd kissed them, touched them, sucked their dicks, and had his dick buried inside their—

Grady forced the thought from his mind. It wasn't like he'd been celibate, not even close.

Only he'd been searching—aching—for something that no amount of fucking women was ever going to satisfy.

Yet he still couldn't shake the conclusion that if he hadn't pushed Mateo away, it could've been just the two of them exploring that new terrain together.

But no... Mateo had done that with someone else. His first fuck with a guy had been with another man.

Grady tried again to kill those thoughts. But curiosity tore away at him. "Why did you break up?"

"I don't want to talk about this." Mateo stormed past him and crossed the room until he was standing at the foot of the bed. He added in a low voice, "Not with you."

Again Grady let that go. For now.

He was about to change the topic once more, but then Mateo asked, "Where do you work?"

"Here." Grady pointed to the drafting table folded up in the corner beside the bed. Whenever he worked on his building plans, he would set the table up in the middle of the room so he had all that natural light pouring in from the picture window. And the view didn't hurt either. Working on his designs at the lake had proved to be one of his best decisions. He was creative here in a way he wasn't anywhere else. "Most of my clients are on the East Coast. It seemed stupid to open an office when I could be working at home most days."

"Thought you were gonna work at your dad's firm?"

"I did for a while. But then I took on some side work, and it grew into a full-time thing."

"That's…"

"What?"

"Impressive. You did a lot in six years."

Grady wanted to tell him how much it meant to hear that from him, but then Mateo asked, "Mind if I take a shower? I stink like the restaurant."

"No. Go for it." Grady gestured to the bathroom door, which led to the only other room in the place.

Mateo snorted out a laugh as he snatched his bag from the chair by the front door. "I remember."

Right. They'd stood in that shower together that day, kissing and touching and rinsing the cum from their skin. Grady was about to offer a tease on what exactly Mateo did remember, but Mateo was already in the bathroom, the door closing behind him.

A minute later the water started running.

Before Grady could stop himself, he was at the bathroom door. An action that had him feeling like a stalker again, but apparently not enough to make him stop what he was doing.

He leaned against the wall beside the door and listened to the beat of the water hitting the shower walls, listened to the shifting feet on the fiberglass tub floor. He was getting aroused just thinking about joining Mateo under the spray of water, seeing if his body looked the same as it had in college, touching all that wet skin, exploring every inch of him with hands and mouth and tongue, doing things they never got to do six years ago.

The water turned off, and he pictured Mateo toweling off, running the terry cloth over his back, his thighs, and his ass.

Grady had a hand flat against the door, trying to talk himself out of twisting the door handle and slipping inside.

The water turned on again. From the sink that time, by the sound of it.

Was he shaving?

Was he wearing only a towel? His underwear? Nothing?

Grady leaned in, resting his forehead on the back of his hand, letting himself fall into the vision of joining Mateo in the small bath, running his hands over the damp skin of Mateo's shoulders, licking at a drop of water that fell from his hair to his nape, pressing his own groin against Mateo's towel-covered ass, reaching around and opening that towel.

The water turned off, and a loud *thud* came from the other side of the door.

"Mateo?" Grady knocked. "You okay?"

Nothing.

"Mateo?" He turned the handle on the door. It was unlocked. He swung the door open.

Mateo was bent over the edge of the bathtub, picking up Grady's shampoo bottle that had fallen to the shower floor. He was barefoot, wearing jeans, no shirt, his hair wet and dripping water onto his shoulders. A toothbrush was sticking out of his mouth.

Grady was transfixed, watching a lone drop of water work its way down the back of Mateo's neck, then along the flushed skin of his upper back.

That was when Grady saw them. Numerous scars—nearly too many to count—crisscrossing Mateo's right shoulder blade. They continued all the way down and across his back. It looked like someone had flogged the hell out of him with a leather strap or a belt or a whip. Three of the scars looked worse than the others, with more scar tissue. They were wide and ghastly. They had to have bled like a son of a bitch when they were new. And hurt something god-awful.

Grady was speechless. He couldn't move.

Mateo straightened and scrambled to return the bottle to the shelf in the shower. He tossed his toothbrush into the sink and grabbed a T-shirt that he hastily tugged on. "I said just a minute." He went to the sink to rinse the toothbrush. He stuffed it and a tube of toothpaste into his bag, then did the same with a can of shaving cream and a razor. Although Mateo hadn't used either of those. He still sported the dark dusting of facial hair.

"I'm starving," he said in a tone way too casual for Grady's tastes. Maybe forced casual, but still... "You hungry?"

Grady hadn't moved yet, couldn't move. Or find the words to ask what the hell had happened to him. He swallowed and found his voice. "Yeah, sure."

"That pizza joint next to the gas station on Riverdale still open?" Mateo asked the question in a rush, like he was trying to cover his unease, or to get Grady onto something else. He picked up his bag and moved to slide past him.

Grady held his ground in the doorway. Mateo would have to physically shove him aside to get by.

He stopped short of that.

"Teo," Grady said, "what the fuck happened to your back?"

"Nothing." Mateo met his stare. "It was a long time ago." He added more as if he knew Grady would never let it drop. "I'm not going to talk to you about it."

"Yeah, you are."

"No." He took a step forward, almost coming in contact with Grady. "I'm not."

The hell he wasn't.

Whatever had happened to him, it had to be the reason he'd been so hard to find. He *had* been in hiding, just like Riley had suggested.

Before they left the cottage that weekend, Grady was getting some answers. Hell, he was getting them before Mateo walked out of the bathroom. He folded his arms over his chest and stared Mateo down.

Even if he had to break his promise and pull out the cuffs again to get Mateo to stay and talk to him, he was going to find out who had hurt him, exactly what the hell they'd done to him, and—most importantly—if they were coming back for more.

Chapter Four

"You walk out now, and you know things will never be the same between us."

Those words Mateo had said to him six years ago kept rolling through Grady's mind as they stared each other down, standing in the bathroom doorway.

Mateo shifted his weight, like he was signaling that Grady better get his ass out of the way or Mateo was coming through anyway.

Grady didn't move. Wouldn't. "Did someone hurt you?"

"Fuck you, Grady. Yeah, someone hurt me. But not as much as you did."

He almost recoiled at that, but he held his ground.

Mateo shook his head. Trying to shake off the painful memories? Or did he want to take back his words?

"What the fuck happened to your back?"

Mateo looked to the ceiling and let out an uneven, ragged breath. His throat muscles worked as he swallowed. "I'm not going to talk about it." He met Grady's stare again. "I need you to respect that."

Despite his words—and the way he'd said them—something had changed in him, like the shower had washed away some of his tension and anxiety. Or maybe it was standing so close to Grady that had him more at ease.

Grady could smell his own soap on him. Another droplet of water dripped from his wet hair to his neck, then slid down under the collar of his T-shirt.

Grady licked his lips, and Mateo's gaze dropped to his mouth.

They stood there, locked in that moment, the silence stretching on between them.

Mateo swallowed hard again, kept watching Grady's mouth. "What made you realize?"

It took Grady a few seconds to process that. "Realize that I was gay?"

"Yeah." Mateo licked his own lips then.

The moisture that swipe of tongue left behind made those lips look softer, fuller. Or it could've been that Grady couldn't take his eyes off that mouth, and the longer he stared, the more the details stood out. He pushed himself to think, to respond. "It was the dreams."

The grunted agreement made it seem like it had been the same for Mateo at one point in his life. Of course it had. Somewhere along the line he'd accepted he was gay, really accepted it, and chose to live his life in that vein.

Not spend it in hiding like Grady, trying to force himself into a straight existence he was never meant to live.

Then again, all the evidence had pointed to the fact that Mateo had been in hiding for his own reasons.

To make sure they were on the same page with what he'd been saying, Grady added, "Dreams about you."

"Stop." Mateo shook his head. "No more lies. The real reason."

No more lies? Did he mean something Grady had said that day? Or six years ago?

He *had* been having dreams about him—the most intense, erotic dreams—but he let that go. He withdrew a couple of steps to give Mateo some space, taking a chance he wouldn't walk away.

"After college I pretty much made a career out of trying to avoid anything that would get me thinking about what I was or wasn't—about what I wanted, about what my dreams were telling me. Then one day…" He shrugged, not sure if he should really go on. Not sure if he wanted to.

Mateo dropped his bag onto the floor beside him and leaned against the bathroom doorway, intently watching him, listening.

"I walked in on two guys in the steam room at my gym. One

was blowing the other. The guy sitting there with his towel open, his dick hanging out, told me to get the hell out or step inside and enjoy the show."

"You stepped inside?"

"Yeah. Jerked off watching them. Hadn't come so fast in a long time. It became a regular thing. Watching the two of them every morning before work. Sometimes they blew each other. Sometimes it was handjobs all around."

Mateo huffed out a brief laugh.

"Yeah, just like the old days." Grady wanted him to say something, anything.

Mateo didn't.

So Grady pressed on. "A couple of weeks later I told my second wife the truth. I knew it wouldn't be long, and I'd be the one on my knees in that steam room, that guy's dick in my mouth. I knew it was a line I couldn't cross, not when I was married to her, but I also knew I would do it. Eventually I'd do it."

"Did you?" Mateo asked the question in a near whisper. He was back to focusing on Grady's mouth. "Have you ever given a guy head?"

"No." Grady met his stare, let him see the slow buildup of anticipation in his expression. "But I will."

Mateo kept studying him. Then he pushed away from the doorway, took a step forward, and another, closing the short distance between them. "You ever kiss another guy? Other than me?"

"No."

That slight smirk was back. He raised an eyebrow, and Grady's breath caught. Mateo moved into his space more and backed him against the wall. He pressed his hands flat to the wall on each side of him.

God, Grady wanted those lips on his. He desperately wanted to grab hold of Mateo and do whatever Mateo wanted, whatever Mateo would let him do until they both came, sweat-soaked and panting, dying to do it all again.

Instead Grady stayed perfectly still and waited. He thought maybe they both needed Mateo to set the pace right then.

Mateo leaned in, then stopped.

The air in the house seemed to thicken, making it harder to breathe, to think.

When Mateo didn't move again, Grady spoke. "I'm sorry, Teo. I'm sorry I was such a fucking coward. I never should've left like that. I was just...scared shitless."

There was a long pause. Then Mateo said, "I get that, but—" He pulled back and turned away. He charged into the living area. Grady almost missed his next words. "We can't go back."

Right. But... "How about we go forward?"

Mateo stopped at the window near the kitchen table, his back to Grady. "How about we get that pizza?"

"No." They were having this out. Right now.

Slowly Mateo faced him. For the first time, there was tenderness and compassion in those dark eyes.

And hope?

Maybe it was time for something else.

Grady approached. "How about we forget the food and do what we both know we want?" He reached down and adjusted himself through his jeans, letting Mateo see how just being that close had affected him. He gave a long stroke through the fabric, then moved his hand away so Mateo wouldn't miss the evidence of his arousal.

Mateo didn't move, didn't speak, but it was clear he was working something out in his head, his gaze locked on the front of Grady's jeans.

Grady kept quiet. Waited.

Another long pause. Mateo's lips parted like he was going to say something. He didn't. A few deep breaths, and then he finally said, "Get on the couch, Grady."

Grady didn't argue. He moved with urgency and leaned back in the middle of the cushions. Whatever Mateo wanted, whatever he'd let them have right then, Grady was ready for it.

Mateo came to the couch, moving deliberately but carefully, like he was afraid Grady would surge up and beat the hell out of him once he figured out what Mateo was doing. Then Mateo sank to his knees before him. "Is the door locked?"

The same thing he'd asked that day.

When Grady said nothing, Mateo asked again. "The door?"

"I don't know. Yeah, I think so."

His hands landed on Grady's knees. They were in exactly the same positions they'd been back then too. Grady on the couch. Mateo on his knees before him.

"Good." He ran those sure hands up Grady's thighs.

Grady could feel the heat of his palms through the jeans. "Teo…"

Mateo stilled his hands, and he threw Grady a smirk. He got his hands moving again. He reached for the button on Grady's jeans. "Just relax." He had the zipper down. "I promise you'll like it." With deft precision he tugged the jeans open.

This was so very different from the man who'd entered the house with him just an hour before. Grady didn't want to think about why Mateo was doing this. Or think about how much experience he had doing this with other guys.

So he didn't think. He lifted his ass off the couch, and Mateo got the jeans and briefs out of the way.

Then Mateo leaned in, his lips parted as he gripped Grady's cock at the base and angled it toward his mouth.

His fucking mouth.

Mateo Alvarez was about to suck his dick.

They had never made it to a blowjob that day. Never made it past kissing and touching and rocking against each other until they came.

He watched Mateo's mouth getting closer and closer. Grady was breathing so hard he had to look like he was having some sort of asthmatic attack. "Are you sure…"

At first all Mateo offered in return was another amused grin. His warm exhales glided across the tip of Grady's dick. Then he said, "Even straight guys like getting sucked off by a gay man."

"I'm not—"

Then Mateo's lips were wrapped around the head of Grady's dick, and all words were gone.

A moist tongue and lips ran along the ridge, pressed at the slit again and again, and then Mateo's mouth encased the entire head in heat. He took him in deeper, and Grady's head fell back to the couch behind him as the sweet suction started.

"Holy sh—" A low groan escaped his chest.

He reached out and gripped the couch cushions on either side of him. He looked down at Mateo again, not wanting to miss a second of this. Mateo's lips were wet with his saliva, his cheeks sucked in as he went to town on him. The strong lines of his face, the dusting of dark facial hair... It was all so very different from watching anyone else do this to him.

Grady had never felt anything like this. He'd had a shitload of blowjobs in his life, but nothing like *this*. He'd never been so ready to come this fast. And he'd never been this connected to someone. So completely in the moment with him.

Which made sense.

This was Mateo.

The person he trusted more than anyone, no matter how many years it had been since they'd last seen each other.

It didn't take long, and he was ready to explode, his hips involuntarily lifting him off the couch so he was going deeper into that beautiful mouth. Mateo was working him over with lips and tongue and a hand in a way that mimicked Grady's own jerking off.

All that time and Mateo hadn't forgotten.

He remembered just how Grady liked to be stroked. The rhythm Grady used on himself when he wanted it faster, how much he liked the twisting corkscrew motions mixed in with the up-and-down tunneling strokes.

Mateo remembered it all. From watching—and listening to—Grady touch himself six years ago.

But Grady wanted more now. The only place they were connected was along his shaft. He wanted Mateo's hands on his balls, stroking the skin behind. He wanted to be naked and on the bed, wanted to be touching Mateo everywhere, and he wanted Mateo's dick in his mouth right then too.

Just that thought did him in.

"Teo—"

Mateo grunted. He sucked and tugged harder.

Grady jerked his hips again, lifting himself off the couch, sending his cock deeper into the wet heat of Mateo's mouth one last time, and he shot. He couldn't stop the low, desperate groans that poured out of his chest as Mateo kept on working him over, kept that suction and heat wrapped around him.

When Grady had given up every last ounce of his release, only then did Mateo drop back on his heels, breathless, his chest rapidly rising and falling, his wet lips parted.

"Kiss me," Grady said—no, more like begged. He'd never wanted that simple, soulful connection with someone more in any other moment of his life.

Mateo sat staring back at him for another minute, his upper body still shifting with each breath. Then in a heartbeat he stood and walked to the bathroom, shutting the door behind him.

The deafening silence left in the wake of that door closing washed away Grady's postorgasm high. And left him disappointed and more frustrated than before the blowjob.

An eye for an eye.

Would he have to endure Mateo walking away at the end of the weekend?

Would he have to wait six years to really touch Mateo again?

Or would he never get that chance?

Chapter Five

An hour later they were sitting on the porch in two Adirondack chairs, nursing a couple of beers and eating the last slices of pizza, saying nothing of what had happened earlier.

When Grady's eyes had adjusted to the darkness, he could see the water roll onto the beach in a slow cadence that almost hypnotized him into thinking he'd already gotten through to Mateo and they were spending a romantic weekend together.

Ridiculous, really, when he thought about it. He'd never wanted to go away on some sentimental, corny holiday with either of his wives. The weddings—and the marriages—had been so rushed there hadn't even been an official honeymoon for either.

And yet here he was…imagining those kinds of moments with Mateo.

If nothing else had convinced him this was the real deal, those thoughts did.

He just had to figure out how to show Mateo he knew that now.

Sitting there on the porch, Grady could hear the rustle of the trees and brush swaying in the wind, the occasional hoot of an owl, and the steady lapping of the water against the side of the boat tied to the dock. No constant whoosh of traffic, no honking of horns. No signs of any other human life. Like the world had faded away, and it was only the two of them. Alone. Together.

Yet not really together. Not yet.

It was a cold night for late September. A storm was in the forecast for the next few days, but nothing was on the horizon yet.

Kind of like what was going on—or not going on—between them. Was there a storm brewing for them too?

Grady glanced over at Mateo and was trying to figure out what to say when Mateo spoke.

"I always loved it here. The quiet—the peace—at night. Yet the main house would be full of people on the weekends. Full of life. I always felt like I belonged."

"You did. You still do."

He seemed annoyed by that. He tossed the crust from his last slice of pizza into the box that sat on the table between them.

"Is that why you agreed to come?" Grady asked. "Because you wanted to see this place again?"

Surprisingly Mateo shook his head. "I owed you."

But there had to be more to it than that. Or was Grady just hoping for too much? Was it too late? Had something changed the way Mateo felt? Or changed him?

"Why were you so hard to find?"

Mateo said nothing. He wouldn't make eye contact, just kept watching the moonlit water slowly wash in and out on the beach.

"You're hiding from someone, aren't you?"

The brief look of shame confirmed Grady had hit on the truth.

"Are you in some kind of trouble?"

Mateo threw him another glance full of indignation like that was the cruelest thing to say to him. "You think I did something illegal?"

"No."

"You wouldn't be the first."

Without giving it much thought, Grady knew what that meant. "Your uncle?"

Mateo's jaw twitched, but he didn't have to explain. Not to Grady.

He could only imagine what Mateo's uncle had said, and that pissed Grady off. More than he wanted Mateo to see right then. Because who was he to have that reaction after he'd been absent from his life for so many years?

"I'll be right back." He reached for the pizza box and carried it inside. He shoved the box into the trash and threw open the refrigerator. Standing there, bathed in the light from the fridge, he sucked in a deep, steadying breath, then took his time grabbing two more beers, trying to cool his temper.

When he returned to the porch, Mateo must not have heard him coming. He flinched as Grady sat.

Fucking flinched.

Whatever had happened to him, it *had* changed him.

"I'm not going to hurt you." Grady held out a beer for him. "I would never hurt you."

Mateo huffed out another laugh and plucked the beer from Grady's hand. Then he sobered and drank a leisurely sip. Maybe the anger was dissipating. What would that leave behind? Pain? Resentment? Affection?

"Why have you been hiding?"

Mateo's entire body tensed, but he sat perfectly still, like he was unable to decide between letting Grady in or taking off and getting the hell out of there. He relaxed and swallowed down a guzzle of the beer. He was back to watching the water. "It's a long story."

Grady nodded, trying not to come off as too pushy or too invested. He wasn't sure what had happened, but he had a good idea that whatever Mateo shared with him, whatever would happen between them, Mateo would need to know in hindsight he'd done it for his own reasons. Not because Grady forced him to.

Grady stood and gestured with a tilt of his head toward the lake. "Come on."

Mateo didn't move.

"Let's go take the boat out."

He looked to the motorboat tied to the dock. "You'll piss off the neighbors."

"Not that one. The canoe."

Mateo watched him for a while. He drank more of his beer, then set the bottle on the arm of the chair and stood.

They got the boat out and onto the water, moving and working without words like they'd never lost touch and had been coming out to the lake together all these years.

They even sat in their usual places in the canoe. Grady in the bow, and Mateo behind him in the stern.

They had the oars situated and were paddling out in no time. They stopped when they reached the middle of the lake, and Grady swung around on his seat so they faced each other.

Crystal Spring Lake was small enough that during the day they'd be able to make out the cottage along the shore. But in the dark, the porch light was just one lone glow in the distance. Mateo stared back at that light like it was all that grounded him to this world, and if he looked away, he'd float off and be lost forever.

"Why were you at the parade?" Grady asked as he handed Mateo a new beer from the stash he'd brought. If Mateo was hiding from someone, Grady couldn't wrap his head around why he'd gone somewhere so public.

The answer came that time without hesitation. "I promised a friend from the restaurant I'd be there. It was his big day, and I didn't want to miss it." He opened the beer and made like he was going to take a drink. He stopped. "He was in drag. His first time."

"Mine too."

Mateo threw him an amused, surprised look.

Grady laughed. "Not in drag. Just my first pride."

"You're out now?" Mateo's expression softened, then went hard again as he focused on the beer.

"I'm working on it. Hell, it's a done deal. I posted all over Facebook that I was trying to find you, and why."

Mateo nodded. He was now glancing over Grady's shoulder at the wilderness surrounding the lake, concentrating a little too hard like he was searching for a ghost traipsing among the maple trees.

Finally he asked, "What did your posts say?"

"That I've never stopped thinking about you."

That had Mateo back to the stoic silence, the trees holding his complete fascination.

Might as well go for broke. Grady added, "That I was in love with you six years ago. That I still am."

There was no reaction, and the disappointment hit Grady hard.

An owl screeched in the distance. The wind picked up speed, and a gust of cool air whipped across the boat. For a moment Grady thought about turning them around and heading back before the temperature dropped even lower. Then sanity returned. There was no way he was breaking the momentum they had going.

He asked, "Did you know about yourself right away after we... After we were here last time?"

Mateo took a swig of the beer as if he had to think before speaking, or work up the courage to share something so personal. "There was no going back for me after that weekend."

Even though Grady had asked the question, the answer stung. He wanted to say something, apologize again, try to get Mateo to understand the dark, confused place he'd been living in back then.

But before he could come up with the right words, Mateo spoke again.

"You really haven't been with any other guys?"

"I haven't." He didn't want to ask, but something inside him needed to hear it. "I guess you have, huh?"

Mateo turned his focus back to the shore, to that lone light from the cottage, and said, "Just the one."

Grady wanted to know more, but again he thought better of pushing it. "That was the best damn blowjob I've ever had."

Mateo raised the beer to take another drink, paused the bottle before it hit his lips. He smiled. "Thanks." He downed the rest of the beer.

"Why wouldn't you let me do the same to you?"

"Because even now you can't say it."

"Say what?"

"That you wanted to suck my dick."

"I wanted to suck your dick."

They stared at each other. The light of the moon bouncing off the surface of the water had Mateo's eyes looking even darker, more intense.

Vegetation rustled somewhere behind him, and a flock of

sparrows took flight from the trees along the shoreline. Mateo swung around in his seat. "What was that?"

"Nothing. They were probably just spooked by a deer."

Mateo continued his surveillance around the perimeter of the lake, then turned back again, more alert than he'd been before the disruption.

If he was going to be that jumpy, maybe the middle of the lake this late at night wasn't such a good idea.

So much for the conversation they'd been having.

Grady tried another tack. "Did you ever get to Mexico?"

Mateo seemed to consider that, or maybe it was Grady's motives he was considering. "Nah," he said.

That surprised Grady. A lot.

Mateo's aunt and uncle had rejected their Mexican heritage long before Mateo came to live with them. They never taught their children—or Mateo—anything about their families' customs or traditions. Hadn't even allowed them to learn Spanish. Not one single word. Mateo had picked up a few slang words here and there, same as all the other boys in school, but that was all. Not speaking the language from where he'd been born had always bothered Mateo. It had been one more thing that had him feeling completely disconnected from the parents he'd never known.

"I thought you were gonna go as soon as you could get the money together."

"Didn't work out."

"Why not?"

Mateo shrugged. Then the barest hint of excitement flashed in his eyes, like when they were kids and it had been time for them to hit the ice for practice. "I've been studying Spanish."

"Yeah? Your aunt and uncle would love that."

"I don't give a shit."

"I didn't say you should. You don't see them much?"

"Nah." He shrugged again, then added, "I don't see them at all."

"Their choice or yours?"

"Both."

Grady nodded, feeling even worse about what he'd done.

Biggest. Asshole. Ever. Did Mateo have anyone he could count on after Grady had walked out on him?

Distant lightning sparked in the dark clouds to the west. Then a low rumble came from the sky, and Mateo flinched again.

They should've headed back long before then. Grady couldn't bring himself to turn around and start paddling.

Instead he asked, "What was your boyfriend like? The one you thought it was serious with."

"He…" When Mateo didn't say more, Grady figured he'd get another admonishment to let that topic go too. Or maybe Mateo would just ignore it.

In contrast to that he continued. "He turned out to be someone very different from who I thought he was." He gave Grady a pointed look. He could've been talking about him, and they both knew it. "He turned out to be…" He paused. "Not a very nice guy. He lied to me about…everything."

"He's the one you're hiding from?"

That time he didn't respond.

"He's the one who beat the hell out of your back?"

Again nothing.

Time for another change. Anything to get Mateo talking again. Maybe then he'd eventually admit how he'd gotten those damn scars.

"Since I saw you at the parade," Grady started, "I've been thinking a lot about college. All that stupid shit we used to do. What total newbs we were when we moved into the dorm. Remember during that first week when we couldn't find the cafeteria?"

That still got no reaction.

They had ripped on each other all through school about that week, one blaming the other for getting them lost every time they went looking for the lone cafeteria on campus.

Grady continued. "That first night we ended up eating that entire tin of snickerdoodles from my mom, a box of raisins, and a bag of fried onion rings from the vending machine, and we were still fucking starving."

Mateo didn't laugh, but his lips turned up at the corners, and the look in his eyes softened once more.

"We asked ten people and still couldn't find the damn building. We even followed that one guy who you swore looked hungry."

Mateo glanced his way. "He *did*."

"Yeah, he was hungry for something, all right. He went straight to a sorority house."

They both laughed.

The laughter died off, and Grady would give just about anything to hear that sound from him again.

He tried another one. "Remember that night our senior year when we got in that big fight over who had the best slap shot on the team? I thought it was me; you thought it was you."

Mateo reached for a new beer, twisted the cap off but didn't take a drink. "It didn't start out as a fight."

"But it sure ended that way." Wrestling on his bed, Grady wearing only a pair of briefs, Mateo in just a jockstrap. "You elbowed me in the face, and I had a black eye for a week."

"I didn't mean to hit you."

"Yeah." He paused, purposely drawing out the moment. "I almost kissed you that night."

Mateo chuckled again at that, shaking his head. "You did not."

Another flash of lightning lit up the sky to the west. The storm was getting closer.

Mateo didn't flinch that time. Just kept studying Grady like he was trying to read him, to see the motives hidden behind the words.

Another gust of wind tore across the boat. The temperature felt like it had dropped fifteen degrees since they'd set out.

Only, Grady wasn't cold.

Not even close.

"I did," he said. "I *wanted* to kiss you. I'd been thinking about it every time we jerked off together. But I was trying to tell myself I wasn't thinking about it at all."

Mateo kept watching him, and Grady stared him down in return, not wanting to break the tenuous connection.

Then Mateo moved with a start. He chucked the bottle of beer over his shoulder to the canoe floor and surged forward, clearing the thwart in the middle with one step, the canoe rocking and nearly tipping over in the process. He dropped to his knees, grabbed Grady by the shirt collar, and dragged him off his seat until Grady was straddling his lap.

Grady's shirt still clenched in his fists, Mateo jerked him closer. "Goddamn you."

Chapter Six

Those two words were barely out of Mateo's mouth, and then his lips covered Grady's.

It wasn't soft or tentative. It was a powerful, consuming kiss, and Grady no longer had to wonder if kissing Mateo would be as intense as it had been that day six years ago.

It was better than he remembered, better than he imagined.

He held Mateo by the back of the head and pressed their mouths together harder. Mateo had his hands on Grady's back, tugging him closer. Grady responded, opening his legs more, moving farther up Mateo's lap. Their mouths opened, and their tongues touched, caressed.

Each contact of Mateo's lips and tongue, and those sure hands holding him against that strong, firm body shot desire blazing through Grady.

This was no gentle embrace or playful teasing. This was power and passion and instinct driving them on.

With his legs spread, his arms wrapped around Mateo, Grady felt open and vulnerable, and yet alive and free and more turned on by Mateo's touch than anything he'd ever known.

The completely foreign brush of Mateo's stubble against his chin had an erotic element to it Grady never would've guessed. He held Mateo's face in his hands and let his thumbs explore that rough surface over Mateo's face and jawline, wanting to feel that stubbly skin rubbing against his own while Mateo was lying on top of him, buried inside him.

That thought had him rocking against Mateo. Grady's hard shaft was trapped between their bodies. The friction—blended with the all-consuming kiss—had his body ready, aching for sweet release.

Then all of a sudden Mateo pulled back. He searched Grady's face. "You're shivering." He glanced up at the clouds and at the lake around them. The night sky had grown darker, more ominous, the thunder louder.

"It's not the cold." Carefully, in order to keep them from tipping over, Grady moved off his lap and shifted them around so Mateo was the one sitting on the bench, Grady kneeling on the canoe floor before him. He ran his hands up Mateo's thighs. "It's definitely not the cold." He went for Mateo's jeans. "And I'm not waiting another minute. I want you in my mouth."

Mateo stopped him. He reached out and cupped his cheek. "Are you sure about this?"

"You have no idea."

A relaxed, knowing grin hit Mateo's lips. It was very different from any other way he had looked at Grady yet. "Yeah, I do." He leaned down and kissed Grady again. This time going slow and easy like he was savoring him, his fingers stroking Grady's cheek. When Mateo pulled back, he had his jeans open, his cock out, his other hand moving over it. "Jerk yourself off while you do it. I want to see you touch yourself with my dick in your mouth."

God, Grady loved hearing Mateo talk to him like that.

A cool drop of rain hit his cheek, but he couldn't care less.

Because right there before him was Mateo's naked, beautiful erection.

Grady took the shaft in his hand, and Mateo let go at the same time, like the passing of a torch. Significant. Meaningful.

He would've laughed if that didn't feel so damn true. This was meaningful in a way sex had never been for Grady, not really. He leaned in. He wasn't timid. He always thought he'd be nervous, unsure what to do. He simply wanted this with everything he was.

He opened his own pants, slipped a hand inside, and did as Mateo had instructed, while at the same time he parted his lips and took the head of Mateo's cock in, savoring the taste and smooth, sleek feel. He swept his tongue all over and around from the tip to the ridge and back up. That move alone had a wave of power rushing through him. He would've thought sucking dick would have him feeling submissive, not the opposite. He went deeper and worked both hand and mouth over the shaft, paying particular attention to the head, wanting to make this so very good for Mateo.

Mateo groaned, and Grady reveled in that sound.

Then Mateo had one of his hands squeezing his balls. Maybe trying to fend off his orgasm. He had his other hand splayed over the back of Grady's head, massaging his scalp. There was strength to that one touch Grady had never felt from anyone before.

Shallow breaths poured out of Mateo. He groaned again. "Oh fuck!" He whimpered. His legs were shaking.

Grady sucked harder, moved faster. He'd heard the wet, slick sounds of a blowjob too many times in his life to count, but knowing that it was his mouth making those sounds, his mouth driving Mateo crazy, making him sound so desperate and lost and found all at once, was intoxicating and sent another rush of power and excitement through Grady.

The rain was coming down harder now, drops splattering on the wooden surface of the canoe and the lake all around them.

Mateo was muttering something incoherent between deep, soulful groans. He gripped the back of Grady's head tighter.

The boat rocked. There was a chance they were about to tip over, but it didn't matter. Grady had waited too long for this.

Mateo let out an unsteady laugh as the boat rocked more. Grady kept going, putting more focus and vigor into his mouth's movements.

The laughter cut off, and Mateo moaned again. He was lifting off the seat now so that he was the one leading the movement of his dick into Grady's mouth.

"I'm gonna..." He sank back to the seat like he was withdrawing.

No way.

Grady didn't let go, just kept his mouth and hand flying over Mateo's cock.

Mateo surged forward and groaned one last time, long and loud. His shaft pulsed, and he shot.

Cum filled Grady's mouth, so much it dripped down his chin. He breathed deep through his nose and swallowed. That intense feeling of power was back and stronger than ever.

He had made Mateo come. With his mouth.

Mateo pulled out. With a hand under Grady's chin, he encouraged him to look up. "Jesus. Your first time and you had my world rocking."

Grady laughed and smacked him on the side of the leg. "You don't think that was the boat?"

"Nope. Not the boat at all."

Grady shifted off his aching knees to sit back on his ass. "So I'm guessing that means I did okay."

Mateo scoffed. "Yeah. You did okay." That look said it had been more than okay. Then he grew apprehensive. "You liked it?"

"Shit, yeah. Stick your hand down my pants, and you'll see how much I liked it."

That got Grady a smile.

He still had a hand inside his pants, but he'd stopped stroking himself halfway through the blowjob, his total focus on Mateo.

Another flash of lightning tore through the sky overhead, and then a crack of thunder. The rain was now pouring down on them, making it hard to see.

Grady tucked himself back into his pants and gestured toward the shore. "We should head back."

"Yeah." But Mateo didn't look like he'd meant that. Maybe he didn't want this moment to end any more than Grady did.

Grady moved up onto his knees and reached out for him, intending to offer another kiss, a promise of what the rest of the night would bring. But at Grady's feather-soft touch to the side of his face, Mateo flinched.

"Jesus." Grady dropped to his ass again. He searched Mateo's face. "What happened to you?"

Mateo shook his head. "Fuck." He ran a hand through his

hair, slicking it back with the rain. "I'm no good for anyone. Not like this."

"That's...that's not true."

"Grady," he said in a low drawl but loud enough to be heard over the rain. "You don't know."

That time Mateo accepted the touch. Grady held his face in both hands. "No matter what that asshole did to you, what he said to you, you are everything I want. No matter what."

Slowly Mateo nodded, like the words had penetrated some lost part of him.

Lightning struck again, and they both flinched. If they didn't get going, they might actually get their asses electrocuted.

"Shit," Mateo said around an uneven chuckle. "Let's go."

"Yeah." Grady moved to the other seat, and they got the oars ready to row.

They were soaked by the time they were back onshore and had the canoe stowed away in the shed. They rushed to the guesthouse, laughing—genuine, blissful laughter—as they stumbled inside. The room was nearly dark with only one lamp on in the corner and the moon shining in through the thin curtains.

They stripped off their shoes by the door, and Mateo was across the room before the door swung shut behind them.

Grady thought Mateo was going for the shower, but instead he suddenly stopped. He spun around and came back to him. He flattened Grady to the wall beside the door, pressing his weight into him. Grady could feel how hard he was again beneath the wet fabric of his jeans.

"I've been thinking," Mateo said.

"You think too much." Grady reached out and ran the palms of his hands over Mateo's chest. He worked those hands under the hem of the T-shirt, feeling the hard ripples of his abs, then up again, over his bare chest that time. He caressed the firm pectoral muscles, wanting to explore every inch of his skin.

Mateo gripped Grady's hands through the shirt and stilled them. "We do this, and I want it all."

Chapter Seven

"That's what I've been saying." Grady bucked up against him, wanting Mateo to move, to let go of his hands and touch him in return.

He didn't. He said, "I want to touch you. *Really* touch you."

"Teo, we're on the same page here."

Mateo leaned farther into Grady's space. He cupped the back of his head and bent forward to slowly, sensually lick a path up the side of his neck. "I want to fuck you."

Grady gasped as Mateo nipped at his skin. "Nothing's stopping you."

As if that wasn't the right response, Mateo shook his head. All at once he let go of him and shifted away. He went to the window by the kitchen table.

Grady's head was spinning from the loss of contact.

Mateo kept staring out the window. He ran his hands through his wet hair, pausing with his palms pressed to the top of his head. He breathed deep, dropped his arms, and spun to face Grady. "You promised me back then that nothing would change us."

"I know."

He huffed out a laugh. "Yeah."

Grady was trying to figure out what he meant by that when Mateo added, "I know you, Grady. This isn't something you can handle. A couple of blowjobs are one thing. I get inside you, and you're going to panic. You're going to realize you've got a man's dick up your ass, and you'll take off again."

That almost had Grady laughing, picturing trying to run out while in the middle of getting fucked.

Getting fucked?

Was he really ready for this?

He met Mateo's stare, and he knew the answer. "I swear to you, Teo—"

Mateo's eyes widened, and then all at once he was coming at him. For a second Grady thought he was going to punch him out or slam him against the wall. Instead he grabbed Grady and wrenched him forward. He had their bodies crushed together in a heartbeat, and their lips connected.

They kissed slower this time, deeper, more tongue, more time, more savoring.

Feeling oddly confident and more certain of what he was doing, what he wanted, Grady dipped his hands inside the back of Mateo's jeans and gripped his ass, tugging him closer.

"Christ, Grady." His name was a whisper on Mateo's lips. Then he kissed him again. The pressure of Mateo's body against Grady's aching dick had him growing even harder.

Mateo's breath hitched as Grady ground his cock against him.

Their lips met again, and they didn't say another word. Grady could feel Mateo giving in to the connection between them even more than in the canoe. Mateo—and his incredible mouth—had Grady more turned on than any woman or any porn or anything he'd ever done.

When they parted, Mateo threw him a slight grin. That old confidence of his had returned. He brought a hand to the front of Grady's jeans. He got the zipper down and slid that hand inside to cup Grady's cock, skin on skin.

Grady arched into it. "Shit," he said as a rush of breath left him.

Mateo started to move his hand, and Grady shifted his hips into that brilliant, warm touch. Then Mateo stopped. He worked Grady's shirt over his head and backed him to the bed. He turned them and dropped to sit on the mattress, pulling Grady to him so he was standing between his spread thighs, Grady's cock eye level with him.

Mateo stilled, waited. For what? Grady to move next?

Despite all Grady's words and thoughts and actions since

they'd gotten to the lake, he was frozen in place, unsure of what to do or say. He didn't want to ruin this moment.

"It's me, Grady. It's just you and me here."

That was all the encouragement Grady needed. One knee on the bed, he leaned down until he was lying over him, pressing Mateo into the mattress. Their mouths came together once more, lips and hands exploring. Grady lifted the front of Mateo's shirt and moved to taste and lick all that skin over the strong, sleek muscles.

He could feel Mateo's resignation fade away completely, as if Mateo was giving in to something he'd wanted for a long time, something he thought he'd never get. Then he seemed in a hurry. He rolled them over, slid between Grady's thighs, and rocked against him. Maybe he wanted it hard and fast and over with quickly before Grady changed his mind.

Getting off like that wasn't what Grady wanted from him.

Okay, it wasn't the only thing he wanted from him.

He wanted to take his time, savor every touch. He wanted to know everything that drove Mateo mad with desire, give him everything he'd been missing since that fucker who'd hurt him. Grady wanted to show him how good this could be for them.

Mateo obviously had other ideas. He sat up and straddled Grady. He reached for the nightstand drawer. Without another warning he gripped one of Grady's wrists and slapped the handcuff on him. He situated Grady's arm above his head so the handcuffs were fished through one of the metal slats of the headboard.

Grady didn't fight him on it. He just said, "You don't have to do this."

Mateo raised Grady's other arm and clicked the cuff around it so he was secured to the headboard.

"I'm not going anywhere this time."

"Sure." Mateo sat back on Grady's thighs.

In that moment, Grady could see how much he'd hurt him, more than he'd thought possible.

Mateo had been in love with him, seriously in love with him, and he'd trusted Grady not to let whatever was going on with them destroy their friendship.

Maybe this was how it had to be for them this first time. So Mateo could let go and know Grady wasn't going anywhere.

But that didn't sit right with Grady. He wanted Mateo to trust him again.

It would just take time. How much? Weeks? Months? Years, even?

But right then, being together after all this time, Grady wanted to touch him, wanted to explore every inch of him. God, how he wanted his hands and lips all over him.

"It's okay, Teo. I'm not going anywhere this time. You don't need to restrain me."

Mateo said nothing. He slid a hand into Grady's pants and released his cock, stroking until it was more on fire than before the handcuffs.

Eyes closing, head thrown back on the pillows, Grady groaned. He opened his eyes and forced himself to try again. "Look at me."

Mateo finally met his stare.

"I...am...not...leaving."

That had Mateo stopped, his gaze fixated on Grady, uncertainty in those dark eyes. Suddenly he rolled off him and sat on the edge of the bed, his back to him.

"Mateo?"

He said nothing. Just kept his focus on the floor before him, head down.

"Teo."

Still nothing.

Grady shifted, but he couldn't get any closer to him.

Eventually Mateo stood. Grady thought he might actually take off, walk out the front door, and leave him there alone, cuffed to the bed like that.

Then just as quickly, Mateo reached for the key to the handcuffs and unfastened one of Grady's wrists, then the other. He straightened and dropped the cuffs and key on the nightstand, then painstakingly considered them like he was trying to talk himself into something. Or out of it.

He squeezed his eyes shut and sighed. The low light from

the moon started to fade as more storm clouds rolled in until Grady could barely see him.

The quiet continued, Grady scrambling for what more he could say. He lay still, waiting, not sure if he should try to touch him or not.

More silence, and then Mateo spoke, his voice straining with emotion.

"I've missed you so much."

With those words, Grady wanted to reach out and pull Mateo down to him, but something told him Mateo needed to make the next move. And maybe Grady needed him to also.

Mateo's gaze locked on Grady's bare chest. "I've missed just hanging with you, doing stupid shit, laughing. I've missed your family. I've missed being here." Something seemed to shift in him, more than when he'd reached for Grady in the canoe or when they'd gotten inside the cottage. He returned to kneeling on the bed, but he didn't touch Grady.

"I've missed you too, Teo. More than I can say." Only he was saying. He'd been trying to say everything that he could think of, more than he'd ever thought he would express to anyone.

They both moved at the same time and met halfway. This kiss was less about passion and more about saying what words weren't enough for.

Then the kisses grew more urgent, more desperate, Mateo straddling him once more.

They were both still wearing their wet jeans. Mateo still had his shirt on. That would never do. Grady gripped the bottom edge.

Mateo flinched and stopped him, pushing his hands away. "Don't."

And then Grady spotted them. Multiple faint scars running across the inside of each of Mateo's wrists.

"Jesus." Grady studied the scars. Not cuts but something else. They were hard to see in the nearly dark room. He looked up and searched Mateo's face. "What—"

"It's nothing." Mateo shook his head. "It's just…no one's…no one's touched my back since…"

"It's okay. I just want to be naked with you."

Mateo breathed deep and nodded.

Grady slowly reached for the T-shirt again. He got it up and over Mateo's head, moving with care and precision. He ran his hands over Mateo's chest, down over his abs, then around to his sides. He paused. "Can I?"

Mateo nodded again. "They don't hurt anymore."

Grady leaned up and kissed his chest, tongued over and around a nipple, breathed in his scent, all while his fingertips swept over Mateo's back—over the smooth, soft skin and the rough, scarred streaks.

Mateo held him by the back of the head as Grady kept kissing his chest, letting his hands and lips say more than he thought he could voice right then.

But he had to know. "Will you tell me about it?"

"I will. But not now. Please, not now."

"Okay." Grady kept stroking and petting and kissing—reassuring touches.

Then Mateo tilted him back so Grady was looking up at him. "I want you." Another kiss, and Mateo withdrew. He stripped away his pants and briefs, then returned to the bed and worked Grady's jeans and underwear down his body, kissing one point after another along Grady's skin as he went, loving on him in a way he hadn't done yet.

Then Mateo was on top of Grady again, lying flat over him. The brush of Mateo's warm thighs and groin and chest against Grady's own was electric. He had to concentrate on each breath that poured out of him just to keep from arching up into the touch until he came.

Their cocks slid against each other as Mateo rocked forward and back.

And here Grady had thought the blowjob had been perfection.

Touching—connecting—like this... There was no going back for him. How could he have denied himself this for so long?

Mateo ran a hand down Grady's chest, slowly, tenderly moving the tips of his fingers over the flesh of each nipple, then lower. Just when he got close to Grady's dick, he stopped.

He came forward again, lying over him. He kissed his way up the side of Grady's neck. Then his mouth was on Grady's again.

Grady clung to him as their tongues met. This time Mateo held Grady's face in his hands and kissed him like he was savoring him. Not like he had a goal in mind, or was working toward getting off, but that just touching Grady again, kissing him, was what he'd been missing from his life, and he'd almost died without it. He was rocking against Grady now, and that simple contact shattered Grady's control. He moved with Mateo, gripping his ass in both hands, helping him align that perfect glide of their bodies.

Mateo seemed to have lost control too.

That was what had been different about him until this moment. He had been holding back, clinging to his pain and anger since Grady had first pushed into his apartment.

Or maybe that was how he was all the time now.

Maybe those scars meant the asshole who'd hurt him had damaged him more than Grady could imagine—and in ways that had irrevocably changed him.

Although, maybe not.

The way Mateo was touching him, kissing him, it was all very reminiscent of that day six years ago.

His Teo was in there somewhere.

"Remember…" Grady started.

Mateo was trailing his lips down Grady's neck again, still rocking against him.

Grady kneaded his ass in both hands while Mateo found the most sensitive part of his neck just below his ear and sucked. Grady arched up and gasped.

"Remember what?" Mateo asked in an amused tone.

"That first day when I caught you jerking off on your bed, and you didn't stop."

He laughed. "And you didn't look away." He was moving lower and lower down Grady's body, lips and tongue teasing and stroking as he went.

"I'd never seen anything so goddamn sexy. The way you

licked your parted lips, the way your slick hand twisted and stroked faster and faster, the way your toes curled as you got close—your big toe first, then the rest."

Glancing up at him, Mateo smiled against Grady's abs. An exasperated chuckle surged out of him. He shook his head. "Shut up and touch me, Grady. Make me come." He moved up Grady's body, and they kissed again.

Both breathless, they were getting close already. Mateo sat up and lunged for the nightstand drawer. "Don't suppose you got lube in here?" He laughed again and came back with a bottle. "Cherry?"

"Uh-huh." That was all Grady could manage with Mateo's hand slathering lube over his cock, then his own, then both of them together. That was too much.

"I'm gonna—"

"Wait." Mateo stretched out on top of him again, bracing himself, lining them up so their cocks found that sweet friction with each of his thrusts.

Grady wanted Mateo inside him, but there was no stopping them now.

"Shit!" Mateo thrust faster against him. His breathing grew more ragged, and then he was coming, and then Grady was too, their sticky release blending with the lube on their skin as they rocked and thrust through the last of their trembles.

After, when their bodies had stilled, they lay there, side by side, naked, sweaty, the roar of the wind and rain penetrating their dark cocoon.

They had humped against each other like a couple of virgins getting off for the first time, and it was better than any fucking Grady had ever done before, even better than six years ago. This time had been less tentative, more powerful.

"That was…" He let out a shuddering exhale. "Shit, I can't believe I walked away from this."

Mateo said nothing. He remained still. His breathing slowed, and Grady could no longer hear him, could only feel him there because their legs were still touching, knee to shin.

"Mateo?"

Still nothing.

Then his leg was gone.

Grady felt him roll to his side, the mattress dipping, jostling Grady and shifting his world with that one move. He held his breath, waiting for Mateo to get up, to say this had all been a mistake, to grab his bag and walk out the door.

But he wouldn't. What they'd just done had meant something to Mateo. Grady was convinced of that.

The way Mateo had looked at him, the way he'd touched him...

Grady mentally scrambled for what else he could say to ease whatever fears or uncertainties had come over Mateo. Grady couldn't stand the idea of not having anything more than this weekend, of not being together like this again.

Fuck the sex—no matter how great it was—he couldn't stand the idea of not having Mateo in his life again. Period.

Then the bed shifted once more, and Mateo's body was snug against him, his right leg wrapping over one of Grady's. His warm hand was on Grady's chest, a soft caress that moved up his body, ran along the side of his neck. He cupped the back of Grady's head. "Kiss me," he whispered, his voice shaking a touch.

They came together again. Effortlessly. Fervidly.

Grady lost count of the minutes—hours—they spent touching, kissing, exploring, learning about each other in ways they'd never done before. Grady encouraged Mateo onto his stomach. He didn't ignore the scars, but he didn't linger his touch there for long. He caressed Mateo's ass, ran his lips over the backs of Mateo's thighs, then his knees, peppering kisses and licks along his calves to the arches of his feet. That had Mateo squirming and giggling.

They didn't speak. Grady let his lips and hands say all he could to him, and Mateo seemed to be doing the same.

Grady wanted to believe he was reading the unspoken words correctly. That Mateo had forgiven him, that this was just the beginning.

Or maybe Mateo thought this was the only time they'd ever get to be together like this. Maybe whoever he'd been hiding from would catch up to him, and he knew, by just being together, he was putting Grady in the path of whatever danger he was running from.

That thought tore at Grady's heart.

Eventually they stilled, Mateo's head on Grady's chest as he said, "No one's touched me like that in a long time." He shook his head. "No one's *ever* touched me like that."

"Teo..." Grady couldn't wait any longer. He raked his fingers through the dark strands of hair curling over Mateo's ear. "I need to know—"

Mateo reached up and stopped the words with two fingers to Grady's mouth. "Not yet. Just let me have this..." He kissed Grady's stomach, brief, soft kisses that brushed his skin again and again. "Just this for a little while longer."

Grady ran a hand over Mateo's hair again. There wasn't much he'd deny him. Not now.

Mateo lifted his head and gestured across the room to the picture frames on the bookcase. "You remember that last home game we played?"

"Yeah." Of course. He'd only stared at that picture for an embarrassing number of hours.

"That was when I knew for sure," Mateo said.

"Knew what?"

Another kiss to his stomach. "That I was gay. And I knew I'd never just think of you as a friend again."

They'd already been jerking off for months by then. But that was long before the weekend they'd spent at the lake.

"Come here." Grady tugged Mateo up to him, and they kissed again, both of them holding on like that contact was all that would keep anything—or anyone—from coming between them again.

Chapter Eight

Grady awoke to a dark room, an empty bed beside him. He checked the clock. It was the middle of the night.

When his eyes adjusted to the dim light of the moon, he could see Mateo standing at the picture window, staring out into the darkness.

Mateo wore only his jeans. His arms were folded across his chest. Even in that low light, the scars down his back were visible. Every time Grady saw them, he had to hold back the rage burning through him. Hold back on the need to pummel the hell out of someone.

When he found out who had done that to him…

He forced the anger down yet again and got up. It was colder inside now, so he slipped on a T-shirt and his jeans. He approached Mateo, slid his arms around Mateo's waist, and kissed his bare shoulder blade. "Couldn't sleep?"

"I heard something."

"Outside?" Grady listened. The rain was still coming down, a steady beat smacking against the porch deck and railing.

Then a loud *thud* came from outside.

Mateo flinched; his body went tight against Grady.

"What—" Grady stopped when another thud penetrated the rain, this time louder.

"Someone's out there." Mateo moved away, got his shoes on, and grabbed a coat hanging near the door.

"It's probably just the boat hitting the dock."

"I'll find out," Mateo said. "Stay here."

"Not on your life." Grady went for his shoes and coat too.

Mateo stopped with his hand on the doorknob, his body

blocking the exit, and his determined stare aimed at Grady.

Grady returned the glare. "Don't fucking be a dick about this, Teo."

"I'm not being a dick. You're staying here."

In all the years they'd known each other, Mateo had never been overprotective of him like this, never told Grady what he could or could not do. Not even when they'd been kids and done some pretty dumb-ass shit that could've gotten them both hurt—or worse.

The thud sounded again, then nothing but the rain.

It was clear Mateo wasn't going to let him out of the house right then. Grady went to have another look out the window and checked the dock. The boat was swung around the wrong way, several feet out of position. It sat almost at the end of the dock and was banging against the right corner post with each gust of wind. Only one line had held, and that was all that was keeping the boat from taking off with the current.

He pointed toward the dock. "See. The lines have come loose."

Mateo came up behind him and took his own look.

Grady went to grab the boat keys from the hook near the door.

Before he had the door opened, Mateo grabbed his arm. "No!"

"Why? What are you worried about? Is someone coming after you?"

Mateo ignored him and made like he was heading out.

Grady stopped him with a hold on his arm that time. "What happened to you?"

"Let go." Mateo shook him off. He got the door open and went outside.

Grady charged after him. The rain was now a downpour, with stinging drops that came at him straight on and smacked him in the face. The lake was swelling, hitting the beach in choppy waves that were very unusual for Crystal Spring Lake. Grady and Mateo were both drenched by the time they reached the narrow dock. Which wasn't good. The temperature had dropped another ten degrees since they'd gone inside earlier.

As they made their way to the boat at the end of the dock, Mateo scanned the shoreline on each side of the two houses and out over the water. He was definitely afraid the noises he'd heard had been about more than the boat coming loose.

It took them a few minutes to get the motor started and turn the boat back around into place, then to fish out each line from where it had fallen into the water and secure the boat again. Grady's hands were numb before they were done.

"Let's get back inside," he yelled to Mateo over the splatter of rain and the wind whipping around them.

But Mateo was at the end of the dock again, staring out across the lake. He either hadn't heard Grady or hadn't cared.

"What are you doing?" Grady called out. When he got no answer, he advanced. "Come on. It's freezing out here."

"It wasn't just the boat. There was a motor before. A car or another boat."

Grady looked out over the water. With the late hour, the clouds dampening the light from the moon, and the onslaught of rain, he couldn't see far, but where he did get a look, there was nothing. "Everyone's asleep. There's no other boat." Grady grabbed his arm and tugged. "Come on back inside before we freeze our nuts off."

"I have to make sure. I *have* to know if he followed me here."

Grady held on tighter and turned him around. "Who?"

Mateo shook his head, jerking away from Grady's touch once more.

"Mateo!" Grady tried again to get him to turn away from the water. "Tell me what happened. Who is coming after you? Who hurt you?"

Finally Mateo spun his way. "You did."

The rain shifted and blasted Grady's face again. He recoiled a step. Not from the rain. "I didn't leave you scarred."

Mateo glared at him. "Yes, you did."

Lightning struck overhead. Grady could almost feel the electricity zip through the air between them.

"I had no one!" Mateo shouted. He jabbed a finger Grady's

way. "Not you. Not your family. My aunt and uncle were done with me. I had no one."

"Do you think letting you go—denying who I really was—was easy for me?"

"Yes!"

Easy? That pissed Grady off. For the first time since he'd seen Mateo again, he felt anger toward *him*. He shoved at him. "Well, fuck you! I was scared. And a coward, I know that, but walking away from you was the hardest thing I've ever done. I've never been so damn lonely. Ached so much."

The rain transformed into frigid, stabbing drops that stung as they hit his face and hands. The coat he wore was soaked through. Mateo's looked about the same. For a moment Grady thought he was getting through to him, so he stood there in the pouring rain and waited, watching Mateo's face.

"*You* were lonely?" Mateo harrumphed. He looked out over the choppy water again. The rain ran in rivulets off the ends of his drenched hair and down the side and back of his neck. "You had your wives."

"No. I had no one."

Grady just barely registered the clench of Mateo's jaw before a fist came barreling at him. The punch didn't make contact, but the speed of it and the air rushing past told Grady there was a lot of power packed into that punch, a lot of anger. Years of pain and resentment had come exploding out with one swing of Mateo's arm.

If Grady hadn't been so damn cold, he might've been able to keep his balance as he flailed backward to avoid that fist.

He also might've been able to keep himself on the dock. His right foot slipped on the damp wooden planks, and he went sailing over the edge. The side of his face smacked into the water first, then the rest of him.

He managed to try for one last mouthful of air before he went under. Too bad he'd timed it all wrong. He didn't so much gulp air as he did water, and then he was sinking under the surface.

When the hell was he ever going to get things right the first time?

Chapter Nine

When Grady breached the surface again, strong arms were around him, tugging him toward the shore. He coughed out water. Then coughed more, his throat burning with each exhale.

Mateo was muttering something under his breath. Unintelligible words he repeated over and over again as he kept them moving.

Grady was far too cold and drained to ask for clarification.

And he'd thought he'd been cold before the dunk in the lake. The water a foot below the surface was still warm from the long summer months, but the frigid breeze that had rolled in with the storm had him shivering in no time.

Wasn't it just technically summer a few weeks ago?

Mateo didn't stop them once they were out of the water. He dragged Grady with him toward the guesthouse, Grady's feet catching the ground every couple of steps in an attempt at walking.

After Mateo got them inside, he kicked the door shut, again without stopping, and crossed the room.

"I'm okay," Grady managed to say.

Mateo didn't respond. In the bathroom he leaned Grady against the wall beside the shower, stripped off his dripping coat, and began looking him over, starting at the top of his head, feeling around with the tips of his fingers.

Grady shoved his hands away. A funny move, considering how much he'd been dying to get Mateo's hands on him for the past three weeks—hell, the past six years. Or was it longer? Had he wanted him since the beginning? Young boys in love? Could a person find his soul mate at the age of six?

Yes, he guessed, he could.

He *had.*

"I said I'm okay."

"Get undressed and get in the shower." Mateo cranked on the water, went for the cabinet in the corner, and yanked out towels.

Grady tried to undo the fly on his drenched jeans, but his cold, wet fingers slipped.

Then Mateo was there again. He cursed under his breath and reached for the button. He wouldn't make eye contact with Grady as he worked on the zipper next, then tugged Grady's soaked jeans down his thighs.

The warm air hitting his damp, icy skin was almost painful. Mateo knelt before him and kept sliding the pants lower and lower.

Grady stepped out of one pant leg, then the other. Mateo looked up at him as he ran his surprisingly warm hands over Grady's calves. He kept those dark eyes locked on Grady's and reached for his briefs, working them down next. Then he stood and stripped off Grady's T-shirt. Without hesitation he got naked too and wrapped his arms around Grady, dragging him into the shower with him.

The warm water had Grady's skin tingling. He was still cold all over, but he wouldn't be for long, not with the way Mateo was stroking him everywhere, massaging the heated water into his skin.

"What the fuck was I thinking?" Mateo's hands were shaking as he kept on caressing Grady, now with light, feathery touches that warmed him more than the water. "You could've hit your head. God, I can't—" He pulled him into a tight embrace and kept those marvelous hands moving. Along Grady's sides, down his hips and thighs, over his ass.

It all had Grady distracted—beautifully distracted. There was no way he was shoving Mateo's hands away now. He relaxed into the sensations and tilted his head back under the warm spray of water. Mateo swept those sure hands through Grady's hair like he was washing it for him. Grady leaned forward into him again. He ran his own hands over Mateo's lower back and pulled him closer.

Sensation was returning to Grady's fingers, his body. He rested his head on Mateo's shoulder, and only then did he remember Mateo had said something. "You can't what?"

Mateo placed a kiss on the side of his head, another beside that spot. Another. "I can't lose you again." He buried his nose in Grady's wet hair, breathing deep like he was taking in the scent of him.

"You're not gonna lose me." To Grady's own ears that sounded a little too reminiscent of what he'd said that weekend back in college. Hollow words?

No, even then he'd meant them. And now... He knew he finally had what it took to back them up.

Another kiss to the side of his head, a warm hand cupping the back of his neck, and Mateo said, "That last weekend we were here... That was the last time."

"The last time what?"

"I was happy. From that hockey game until the last day we stayed here—those few months when I knew what I'd been feeling was about more than sex, when I knew I was in love with you—that was the last time I remember feeling truly alive."

Grady turned and spoke the words against the skin of Mateo's neck, holding on to him. "Why? What happened to you, Teo?"

A new tension was building in Mateo's body.

Grady waited, holding perfectly still.

Mateo pulled back. "The water's getting cold."

It was, so Grady didn't argue. As much as he wanted to stay in that shower and force the words from Mateo.

They got out and dried off, each wrapping a towel around his waist.

Steam had filled the small bathroom. The heat and the fogged mirror made the room seem even smaller.

Or maybe it was what they were about to discuss that had Grady feeling like the walls were closing in. No matter how much he needed to know what had happened to Mateo.

Grady leaned back against the edge of the vanity. "If you tell me what's going on, I might be able to help. Riley's a deputy sheriff now. If you're in danger—"

Mateo glared at him. "I don't need another cop telling me what to think." He unfolded his arms from his chest and shook his head as if he had to clear away his thoughts, clear away the anger. "Let's not do this here. Get dressed. I'll get you a blanket."

"No!" *Fuck that.* "Now, Teo."

Mateo met his stare again. He must've seen how serious Grady was. He sighed and sat on the edge of the tub. Still wearing the towel, he had his elbows propped on his bare knees, hands clasped in front of him, his gaze focused on the green-and-pink floral bath mat under his feet. It was a casual stance, but one filled with an edgy apprehension.

"I thought—" He stopped and clamped his mouth shut, but then a moment later he continued. "I thought he loved me. I thought I loved him. In the beginning, anyway."

Right. Of course he did.

Yet that stung to hear. Grady held very still and listened.

"When I went to start law school, I met him at the campus bookstore. Sergio Vannelli. He was my age. Just starting there too." His expression grew almost mournful. "And he was beautiful. He looked like someone who could've been on the hockey team with us. I helped him find a book he needed, and we got to talking, went for coffee that afternoon. He came from a huge, close-knit family—like yours—and he'd just been dumped by a guy. I could relate."

Of course he could.

Grady kept quiet, kept listening. He tried very hard to be what Mateo needed right then. Even if he wasn't sure what that was. Listening had to be the first step. It also didn't hurt that every fiber of his being needed to hear this.

"At first we were just friends. I was too..." Mateo glanced up for the first time since he'd started talking.

"Too heartbroken?"

"Yeah." He went back to focusing on the god-awful bath mat. "For weeks we hung out whenever we could. I was studying a lot, and my free time was almost nonexistent. So was his. I never saw him on campus except when we had plans to meet up. By the time I found out he wasn't a student there, we were sleeping together, and I was already—" He stopped.

"In love with him."

"I thought so. At least I did then. But now…I think maybe I just didn't want to be alone. I liked being wanted by someone. It kept me from seeing who he really was."

I liked being wanted by someone.

As hard as that was to hear, Grady was certain the rest would be worse.

"He'd met me in that bookstore on purpose. He was scouting me. His family was expanding their business, and they wanted to hire someone who could blend in and distribute their merchandise on campus and around that part of the city."

"Merchandise?"

He gave a look that said the answer should've been obvious. "Marijuana. Cocaine."

That hadn't been obvious, at least to Grady. "Why did they target you?"

He shrugged but answered despite that. "Because I didn't have a criminal record. I was a law student without a rich family backing me—without any family at all—so they knew I was both smart and seriously needing the cash. The campus also had a pretty significant Hispanic population. Guess they thought I'd seem approachable to the entire student body."

"Did you—" Grady stopped and instantly wished he could take back those two words.

"Take the job? No." He didn't seem offended Grady had asked. He continued. "When Sergio finally told me what he did for a living, I believed him that he didn't want our relationship to end, that he'd go back and tell his uncle that I said no on the job and that I promised not to go to the cops. He said he would confess his love for me to his family, and that I'd be safe, protected even."

"You stayed with him?"

The shame that flashed across Mateo's face nearly broke

Grady's resolve to keep his distance so Mateo would continue talking.

"I thought I could look past what he'd done before we met. I figured he'd been pressured into it by his family, groomed for that business all his life. He promised me he was done with it." He shook his head. "Even then, I think a part of me knew he wouldn't just walk away, but—" Abruptly he cut off. Without another word, he stood and moved by Grady out of the bathroom.

Grady scrambled to follow, still clad in only the towel. "But what?"

Mateo went for his bag and pulled out jeans and a T-shirt. He ditched the towel and got dressed.

There was no missing the analogy of that action. He was closing himself off from Grady, and he hadn't even gotten to the part where someone had whipped the hell out of his back. Or what had caused the scars on his wrists.

"Teo."

He balled the towel up and chucked it at his bag. He stared at where the towel rolled off the bag onto the floor. Then he nodded and crossed the room to the bed. He sat on the edge, moving slowly then, like a man in a trance, or one who couldn't believe he was talking about something he'd held close to him for so long. "At the time, I didn't realize it, but I chose to ignore my gut. I *wanted* to believe him." He glanced up at Grady. "After it was over, I couldn't stop thinking about what a fucking asshole I was. I fell for one guy's lies. Then I did it all over again."

Grady couldn't hold back on that. He surged forward. "Wait. I did not—"

Mateo held up a hand. "I know. I get it now. You told me the truth about what you felt. Your head just wasn't ready to go there." He kept his hand up between them for another moment like he didn't want Grady to move any closer.

Eventually he dropped his hand to the mattress and gripped the sheet in his fist. "When I realized he was still in the business, I broke it off with him. He didn't take it well. He just sat there at my kitchen table, not saying anything, the anger building. Then he stood, real calm, casual, like he was just gonna leave. But then he came at me. He was crazed, fuming. I shoved him away, and he started trashing my apartment. I went for the phone, but he stopped me before I made it. The next thing I knew, I was bound and gagged and in his trunk. When the blindfold came off, I was hanging from an overhead pipe in an abandoned textile factory, my wrists already bleeding from the ropes."

Mateo lifted his hands to his lap and stared down at the faint marks across both wrists. "They only scarred on the insides, which I guess is good. Makes them easier to hide." He was talking in a very detached tone like it had happened to someone else, and that hurt Grady to hear more than if Mateo had been screaming or crying or both. How far did he have to shove the pain down in order to go on living?

Mateo continued. "Sergio's uncle and two other men showed up with a younger man, maybe eighteen years old. He'd stolen from them, and they said it was time for his punishment. They forced me to watch. Sergio stabbed him in the gut, the chest, and the groin, and then they just stood there and watched that kid bleed out on the concrete floor."

"Jesus."

He nodded, swallowed, and continued. "He told me he'd kill me just like that if I said anything to anyone about him or his family's business. Then I guess to hammer his point home, he beat the hell out of me. He tore a loose belt from one of the old machines nearby and used that on my back for good measure. Then they picked up the dead body and took off, left me there. A homeless man found me the next morning. I was still hanging from the pipe, passed out, blood dripping down my back."

Grady's stomach rolled. He turned away and stormed over to the kitchen, around the table, then kept on going to the other side of the room again, kicking Mateo's discarded towel out of his way in the process. God, he wanted to punch the hell out of something—someone.

What an ass he'd been, handcuffing Mateo against his will, forcing him out here to the middle of nowhere like a prisoner.

He couldn't imagine how freaked Mateo had to have been when he'd agreed to come.

But that also meant…

Mateo had trusted Grady. After all this time, his instincts, or maybe his recollections of those years of friendship, told him he could still trust him.

Grady moved to sit on the arm of the couch to keep from pacing more. "Why did they…" He couldn't finish the thought.

"Let me live? I don't know. Maybe he never imagined I'd have the guts to turn him in."

"But you did?"

"Yeah. In the hospital, I told the cops everything. Guess the feds had been working for years to build a case against Sergio's family. For a lot more than what I witnessed. I was all set to testify, to add my story to their evidence."

Something clicked for Grady. "Shit. The Vannelli crime family. I remember hearing on the news a few years ago that several family members were arrested. But they never went to trial."

"Right. They were released on bail. Before the trial started, there was an explosion at one of their warehouses. It killed all four men who were at the factory with me that night."

More details from the news stories were coming back to Grady. Only one of the men died in the explosion. The other three were burned to death in the resulting fire. It was presumed the Vannelli family had arranged to kill four of their own to make sure none of them made a deal with the feds.

"If they're all dead, then who's coming after you?"

Grady got another one of those looks like he'd just asked the stupidest question.

"Sergio. He's alive."

"How? The news said they identified them with dental records."

"I'm guessing someone was paid off to provide those results. Somehow Sergio got out of that warehouse without being seen, and maybe someone else went in before the fire. One of their dealers. A homeless man. I don't know. The feds don't believe me, but I know the truth. Sergio didn't die that day."

"You've seen him?"

"Not exactly."

An uncontrollable panic was rising in Grady's chest. "How do you know for sure?"

"I came home one day about four months after the explosion, and I just knew. He'd been inside my apartment. He'd gone through the papers on my desk. He'd been on my computer. He'd been in my bed."

"But..."

"What?"

"That was almost four years ago, Teo. If he was really alive, wouldn't he have come after you long before now?"

"Not if he wants to ruin my life. This way, I have no idea when or where or how he's coming for me. When I figured out he'd been in my apartment, I left school and moved. He found me again. That's when I went off the grid, got as lost as I could, never staying in one place too long. I paid a tech firm to erase my identity as much as possible so he couldn't trace me through—" He stopped like he wasn't sure he should go on, but then he did. "So he couldn't trace me through anyone I knew or anyone from my past. That was three and a half years ago, and he hasn't found me since." He paused again, then added dryly— too dryly, "But he will. Eventually he will."

The truth hit Grady then. The map in Mateo's dump of an apartment. The notations and photos. "You're trying to find him first."

"Yes."

"Why?"

"I want him to pay for what he's done. I want my life back. I don't want to spend it waiting for him to find me, waiting for him to make his move."

"Why weren't you put into protective custody?"

"To the feds, he's dead. Everyone I was supposed to testify against is dead. There was nothing to protect me from. They didn't believe me that he was alive. They said I was just in shock, that I was imagining things."

"Jesus." Grady stood, unable to keep still any longer. "Why didn't you leave? Why didn't you go to Canada? Or Mexico?

Or anywhere? Why the hell did you stay in the city?" He got moving again, pacing the short length of the room in front of the windows this time.

"Stop, Grady."

He stopped.

"Come here."

He went to the bed, and Mateo pulled him down to sit beside him. Grady gripped the edges of the mattress in both fists, unable to hold back on the anger, on how very pissed at himself he was for leaving Mateo to deal with something like that all on his own.

Even if Grady hadn't been ready for more than friendship back then, he never should've walked away from him. Mateo had deserved better than that.

"Grady..." Mateo reached out and swiped the pads of his fingers over the back of Grady's left hand. He kept stroking until Grady let go of his death grip and turned his hand over.

Mateo slipped his fingers between Grady's and held on. "There's something else—something I should've told you when you first showed up at my apartment."

Chapter Ten

Grady stared at their entwined hands—the one point that connected them—and waited for Mateo to say more.

"I saw your post on Facebook. The one about me. It's how I knew to look for the ad on craigslist. I saw the suggestion about trying to find me there."

Grady glanced up. "You're on Facebook?"

"I sent you a friend request the week after graduation."

"You did not." He would've remembered that.

"I did. But since back then I didn't think you'd accept if you knew it was me, I used the name of one of the guys from our old hockey team." Mateo looked almost embarrassed.

Grady threw him an amused smirk. "Sneaky bastard."

Mateo smiled too, then grew pensive again. "I saw those birthday pictures your mom always tags you in every year. The Fourth of July ones from here at the lake. Thanksgiving. Christmas. I saw your wedding pictures too. Both times."

At those words Grady thought of what it would've been like if their positions had been reversed, how seeing Mateo with his new bride—smiling, wearing his wedding tux, cutting the cake with her, dancing with her, kissing her—how every pixel of those photos would have felt like daggers in his chest.

Mateo added more. "I saw when your statuses turned curt and more infrequent after each divorce."

That was because Grady had felt like a failure after each one. He forced the thought away and laughed at Mateo's confession. "Stalker."

Mateo laughed again too. "Yeah."

"Why didn't you say anything? Especially after what

happened to you? I would've kept my mouth shut about why you were hiding."

He shrugged, but he didn't release Grady's hand. "Because I didn't know how to let you go. Didn't know how to just be friends." He stroked his thumb over Grady's. "I was so angry, but I ached without you—without your friendship. It had been a part of me nearly all my life."

"Teo..."

One long look between them, saying nothing and yet everything at once, and Grady knew what they were about to do. He was sure Mateo did too, and just thinking about it was familiarity and comfort and desire and passion like Grady had never known before.

He gave a squeeze to Mateo's hand, turned away, and stretched out over the bed to reach for the nightstand drawer. The towel slipped off as he moved. He pulled out the box of condoms and the lube—anal lube—he'd bought in a rash moment of hope. He set everything on the bed near the headboard.

"You know," Mateo said around a laugh, "you're killing me here with all this romance."

"Don't tell me you don't want to fuck me." Grady remained lying on his stomach. He lifted his ass in what he hoped looked like an invitation, not some kind of spasm. "Because that will be the first time you've lied about how you feel about me." Warm hands caressed his ass, and then Mateo was lying stretched out on top of him so they were touching from calves to shoulders.

Mateo was still dressed. He ran his lips up the side of Grady's neck. "I want you to know one thing first."

Grady arched up so his ass was pressing against Mateo's groin, and they both groaned.

"What?" Grady managed to ask.

Mateo thrust his hips forward, rubbing his clothed cock along Grady's ass. He kissed the side of Grady's neck again, the scratch of his facial hair teasing Grady's skin. Grady had his own five-o'clock shadow now, and when he turned his head and they kissed, the blend of soft lips and scrape of stubble was incredibly erotic and alluring, and Grady didn't want it to end.

But Mateo pulled back. He licked his lips. "I love you. I never stopped."

Until those words were in the air between them, Grady hadn't known exactly how much he'd needed to hear them.

Before he could say anything, Mateo moved to lie beside him. "I've been waiting so long for this. You have no idea."

Grady turned to face him. "*You've* been waiting?"

Mateo reached for him. He rolled them until Grady was on top. "Yeah, I have." He pulled him down for another long, deep kiss.

Grady sat up, straddling him, and got to work on Mateo's clothes.

Once they were both naked, they were back in each other's arms. They rolled in the sheets, kissing and rubbing and touching as they'd done before, but now with a determined fierceness to it. It was like Mateo thought this was the last chance they'd get to be together like this—the only chance he'd have to fuck Grady.

But that couldn't be true. Not after what he'd just said.

No matter what, Grady wasn't letting him walk away from this.

He would've said something, but Mateo surged up and rolled off him. "Turn over."

Grady didn't think. Just turned over onto his stomach again. Instinctively he spread his legs, his cock pleasantly trapped between him and the mattress.

Mateo ran a hand over his ass. "Perfect."

There was a long pause, Grady waiting, unsure what Mateo would do next. Get the condom on? An unfamiliar nervousness rushed through him. He forced it down. He trusted Mateo, and he knew Mateo would never hurt him.

Then his ass cheeks were being spread open.

"This is what you said you wanted, right? In your ad on craigslist?"

There was a rush of warm air in the most sensitive part of

Grady's ass. Then something hot and wet was doing delicious, swirling things to him.

Mateo's tongue.

Grady buried his face in the mattress and let out a muffled groan. Nothing had ever felt like this.

No sex. No blowjob. Not the experimenting he'd done with his fingers. He'd never imagined *this* could be so sensual, could get him even more turned on than he was, his balls set to explode already.

Then it all came to a crashing halt.

Grady couldn't help himself. He raised his knees under him so his ass was more exposed to the air—to Mateo behind him.

"Fuck." Mateo exhaled the word. "You're so goddamn beautiful." He went back to running that tongue over and around the entrance to Grady's body. All while he massaged Grady's ass cheeks in both hands. Then he slipped a hand forward between Grady's legs to tease his cock.

Grady's body was on fire. Everywhere. He ached. He wanted to come, but he didn't want this to end yet. He was squirming and moaning like he'd never done in his life. He would've been embarrassed about that, but this was Mateo.

He moaned again, louder, longer, wanting more. The ache was growing, spiraling out of control. He wanted Mateo inside him. He punched at the mattress, bit the sheet between his teeth.

Mateo's tongue kept moving on him, in him, never repeating the same pattern, keeping him guessing and wanting and needing.

"Teo! I need—"

Mateo kissed his way up Grady's ass to his lower back, placed another kiss on his flesh, and another until he was lying over him again. "What? What do you need?"

"Please fuck me."

Another kiss to his nape and Mateo whispered in his ear, "Turn over."

Grady did, and Mateo leaned in and kissed him, swiping a tongue across his lower lip. Then he rolled them as one so Grady was on top, straddling his thighs.

With a slight shake to his hands, Mateo got the condom on

himself and lubed his cock, his breath hitching as he ran his palm over himself. He touched Grady's ass next, this time with slick fingers teasing him, stretching him. Who knew that could feel so wonderfully sexy and leave him begging for something hard and hot to fill him?

Then Mateo was encouraging him to move up his body, positioning him over his cock. Mateo's voice sounded more than a little strained when he spoke. "When I press in, you push out. It'll feel weird at first, but trust me, it's better that way."

Grady did trust him. Implicitly. More than any woman he'd been with, and he was in a far more vulnerable position here.

Then Mateo's cock was pushing at his entrance, and despite that trust, panic rose. "Teo…"

"It's okay, Grady. I've got you. Look at me."

He did, and everything clicked into place—all that blinding desire blazing through him, all he felt for Mateo overriding everything else.

"I've got you." Mateo lifted his hips and entered Grady, rocking in slow, tantalizing movements.

"Holy shit."

Mateo stilled. "You okay?"

"Yeah. Yeah, don't stop."

He moved again, and Grady braced himself on the mattress on each side of Mateo. He rocked into that touch, wanting to get Mateo deeper. He moaned, sounding and moving with wanton abandon like the virgin he was—exploring and basking and trying very hard not to catalog every new sensation. He wanted to fall into this moment, lose himself in the pleasure—lose himself in Mateo. He didn't want this to be about fucking.

Well, not just fucking. But about feeling and knowing and watching Mateo lose his mind with pleasure because he was inside *him.*

Grady sank onto his cock again and again, and Mateo fucked him from below, thrusting up into him with what felt like barely contained restraint.

"God, Teo. Fuck me!"

And Mateo did, moving faster with each slide of his cock into him, his hands grasping at Grady's sides, groans tearing out of him at the drive of their bodies coming together.

Grady couldn't stand to wait any longer. He reached for his dick and started jerking himself.

Mateo stopped his hand. "Not yet. I'm going to come inside you first. Then…" The corners of his mouth turned up, and his gaze locked on Grady's as he kept slamming up into him. Grady couldn't decide if he liked it better when Mateo pulled back or when he pressed in.

There was no way he could hold out much longer. Everything was too intense. His body ached more and more with every thrust.

But there was also no way he was missing whatever came next—whatever else Mateo wanted to do with him.

Their combined moans and grunts and the scent of the lake and sex and that undeniable aroma that was Mateo surrounded Grady.

Then there was the sound of Mateo groaning delicious, dirty words under his breath as his body stiffened. He thrust up again and again with little snaps of his hips. His abs contracted, and then he shuddered and came inside Grady.

When his body finally stilled, he dropped back to the bed. "Fuck."

"Yeah." Grady's voice was tight when he spoke. "We definitely fucked."

That had Mateo laughing. He pulled out of him, tugged Grady up his body, and slid down the bed at the same time until Grady was straddling his chest. In one swift move, Mateo lifted his head and took Grady's cock in.

Grady fell forward, holding himself up with his hands braced on the mattress above Mateo. "Goddamn. That's—" But the words were gone.

Mateo jerked the base of Grady's erection as he attacked the head with his lips and tongue, that moist touch dragging across the slit, laving along the underside of the ridge.

Then his fingers were sliding along the sensitive skin behind Grady's balls. He pressed a finger into his ass, reminding Grady of how Mateo's cock had just been buried inside him. That clever finger curled and tapped his gland, and a blast of pleasure shot through Grady. He felt like he was coming already, but he wasn't. Not yet. Mateo kept sucking. He pegged that glorious spot again. And again. And again.

"Fuck!" Grady thought he might lose his mind. "Teo—" His hips surged forward. "I'm gonna—"

And he did.

And Mateo swallowed it down, his lips tightening around him.

Grady's body trembled uncontrollably, and he thrust into Mateo's mouth again and again as Mateo milked the last of his cum out of him.

Eventually he came down from the high of the orgasm, and Mateo released him, rolling them onto their sides. But he didn't give up the contact. He stroked Grady along his back and side. Mateo's breaths sounded as ragged as Grady's.

When he could manage it, Grady sucked in a long inhale. "Holy fuck… That was…that was…"

"Incredible? Mind-blowing? The best sex of your life?" There was a teasing bravado to Mateo's words.

Grady sat up and leaned over him. "Don't fucking joke about this."

Mateo reached up and cupped his cheek. "Not joking. I'm just…" He dropped his hand to his chest. "I guess I'm afraid."

"I'm not going anywhere." Grady lowered his head to Mateo's chest and snuggled in, a leg thrown over Mateo's. "Absolutely nowhere." He ran a hand over Mateo's warm skin. "What do you think? Half an hour and we can go at it again?"

Mateo laughed.

"Hey, we've got a lot of years to make up for."

Another laugh. He caressed the back of Grady's head. "You liked it?"

Grady sat up and stared down at him again. "Were you even listening to me when you were inside my ass? Did you feel how goddamn hard I just came?"

"Yeah, I felt it." Mateo shook his head. "God…I've never felt this good." He stretched and let out a long exhale. "That was ten years of frustration in the making."

"Ten years?" That meant he'd wanted this since their freshmen year of college.

"Yeah, ten years." He encouraged Grady to lie on his chest again, Mateo's hand back to petting and stroking Grady's head and nape.

"You wanted me all that time?"

"Yes. But I tried to tell myself I didn't."

"Why didn't you say anything?"

"What? Lose my best friend even earlier?" His tone was light and teasing, despite his words.

Grady shifted off him and elbowed him in the side. "Don't joke about that either."

As if he couldn't stand the separation, Mateo moved into Grady's arms, with his head on Grady's chest that time, his fingertips sweeping over and around the light dusting of hair covering Grady's pectoral muscles. "How about I'll stop teasing you after six years?"

Six years, and the two of them still together? Still spending the weekends in bed like this?

That sounded just about perfect to Grady.

Mateo pressed a soft kiss to his chest. "How about a shower? Then sleep?"

The scrape of a branch hitting the window over the bed startled them both.

Mateo tensed in his arms.

"It's just that big oak tree with the swing."

"Okay." He relaxed into him again.

They showered, slept, woke up with the sun, and made each other come again, lying sixty-nine-style on their sides.

The storm had passed, and they spent the day in bed, getting up for food and drinks and bathroom breaks. Fucking each time they'd recovered enough to get it up again. Blowjobs and handjobs and kissing and touching and exploring, like they were trying to pack six years' worth into one weekend.

They ate an early dinner naked on top of the sheets. They skipped dessert, instead moving into each other's arms again, kissing and stroking and loving on each other until Mateo was buried in Grady's ass again, Grady sounding even more wanton and shameless than the first time.

And Mateo...

He seemed more free and open than he'd been yet. Like telling Grady about his past had healed a lost, damaged part of him.

Grady wanted to find a way to heal all of him—no matter how long it took.

* * * *

They napped, and by the time Grady awoke, the sun was setting. The window beside the bed was open, and the breeze off the lake was cool but enticingly warmer than the day before. Golden streams of light from the setting sun danced across the rumpled sheet draped over his lower body. The curtains billowed out with each gust of air, mesmerizing him. He lazily stretched and rolled over. The bed was empty beside him.

Fear gripped his chest.

Which was silly. Mateo was probably just making something to eat or in the bathroom.

That realization didn't stop Grady from bolting upright. The rest of the room was as empty as the bed. "Teo?"

No answer.

He got up and pulled on a pair of jeans. "Mateo."

Still nothing.

The bathroom was empty too. Grady grabbed a sweatshirt, tugged it and his tennis shoes on, and ran out onto the porch.

With the bright sun setting over the lake, casting the foreground in dark shadows, it was hard to see anything.

As his eyes adjusted, he spotted the lone figure sitting in the sand, looking out over the water.

He breathed a sigh of relief and went to sit beside him. "You okay?"

"Yeah." Mateo had his arms folded, elbows propped on his bent knees. He had shaved, and he looked very much like he did in college, as if the facial hair had hidden the true man beneath. He kept his gaze locked on the surface of the water that was shimmering in golds and reds and oranges. The breeze picked up, and the air felt cooler out by the water.

"Let's go sit up by the fire pit. I'll get a blaze going."

"I'm not cold." He lifted his face into the breeze. "I feel alive here like I haven't felt in years. I feel..." His eyelids lowered, and he smiled, a peaceful, contented grin that barely moved his lips. Most people wouldn't even have called it a smile, but Grady knew better. "I feel safe."

Grady wanted to believe it wasn't just the place. That it was being there with him.

But then Mateo's mood changed, grew more reflective, withdrawn. "It's time I stop hiding. If I make it so he can find me, and he shows his face, I can prove to everyone he's still alive. I can get the feds involved again." He nodded. Like he'd made a decision. "I have to end this."

"No. Not like that."

Mateo looked Grady's way. He searched his face. "I can't give you what you want me to give. Not yet. I can't let you—" He stopped, let out a long breath. Without another word, he got up and walked toward the water, stopping just before getting his shoes wet.

Grady followed and went to stand in the surf before him. "Can't let me what?"

"I'm not dragging you into this. I can't have you in my life until I'm sure he's not coming back, until it's over. I will not let him hurt you. No matter what I have to do." He paused, then spoke again as if he was talking to himself rather than Grady. "After I find him, turn him over to the feds, then we can..." He didn't finish the thought.

There had to be a better option. Grady considered that, and then something else hit him. What if Sergio had seen his Facebook post or the craigslist ad? What if he had followed them to the lake? Had there been something to Mateo's concerns that he'd heard someone the night before?

Shit.

Grady shot a look over Mateo's shoulder at the guesthouse behind them, then at the road leading away from the house through the trees.

What were the chances?

It only made sense if Sergio knew about Grady's past with Mateo and had been monitoring Grady's activity online. His Facebook page wasn't locked down, so anyone could've viewed what he'd posted.

But who would go so far as to stalk him online like that?

From what Mateo had described, Sergio sounded crazy enough to do it. Grady's gut churned at the thought that he had put Mateo in jeopardy just by trying to find him, by trying to rekindle what they'd had.

He met Mateo's gaze. "Sergio doesn't know about the house here, right?"

"Yeah. I never mentioned this place."

"What about me?"

"He knew about you, but I never told him your name."

Grady breathed deep in relief. "Good. Then you're safe here right now. We can take some time, figure out what to do. I can call Riley and get his ass out here to help us. We'll figure out something that doesn't put your life in danger. We'll hire someone to find this guy, hire a dozen private investigators if we have to."

Mateo said nothing.

"Let's just talk to Riley and see what he suggests. You can trust him."

Mateo watched Grady for another minute, then started ambling along the beach like he was just out for a stroll. Grady stepped in line beside him. When they reached the end of the beach area, they kept on going, walking in the grass along the pebble-covered shoreline.

They didn't speak for a while. Grady didn't push. No matter how badly he wanted to tell Mateo his plan for Sergio to find him was a shitty-ass one and that there was no way he was about to let him go through with it.

Finally Mateo nodded. "Okay. We'll talk to Riley."

The weight pressing down on Grady's chest eased. They kept strolling side by side, the sun disappearing behind the horizon, the last of its light losing its brilliance.

Eventually Grady cleared his throat and asked, "Why did you stay? Why didn't you just leave?"

"It didn't feel like the right move." Mateo shrugged, hands in his pockets. "I was waiting."

"Waiting for what?"

"You."

Grady stopped.

Mateo did too. He gave him a long look. It was loyalty and devotion and maybe something more all rolled into one. "I had to make sure that if you ever figured things out and wanted to try again, I could be with you and not put you in danger."

It all came crashing down on Grady.

Mateo had been living the way he had—hiding and putting himself in the path of a psycho by just trying to find the guy, instead of moving somewhere safer—on the off chance Grady would one day accept that he was gay.

"I knew—especially after Sergio—that you were the one for me, the only one I wanted to spend my life with. I couldn't give up on that, no matter how slim the chance." He held Grady by the waist and pressed their foreheads together. "But I was supposed to find him before this. So you'd be safe."

Grady pulled back. "God, you're so stupid sometimes. And frustrating as hell. You don't have to do this alone. You never did. You could've come to me. No matter what, I would've been there for you."

He seemed to be considering that. "Yeah, but I needed it to be your decision to see me again." He snorted out a brief laugh. "When I saw you at the parade, I couldn't believe it."

"Why'd you run from me?"

"I wasn't sure if you were there for the reason I wanted you to be there. Or maybe you were just supporting a friend or passing by. And when I actually saw you, I was…"

"Hurt. Angry."

"Yeah. And by the look on your face, you weren't there to find me."

"But once I saw you, I was a man on a mission."

"To get laid?"

They laughed.

"That was the reason I went there, yeah, but you screwed that plan all to hell by just standing there, looking so fucking hot."

Mateo laughed again, almost like he didn't believe Grady. Or maybe it had been a long time since he'd thought of himself in those terms.

It was harder to see his face now. Darkness was descending, but Grady had never felt lighter. Even if they had to hide out forever, he'd made the only choice he could, the only one he wanted to make.

Without saying anything more, they made their way back to the beach and into the house, into bed. Grady slept curled around Mateo that night, wanting to keep him safe, keep him there at the lake house where no one knew where he was, and where every problem or worry seemed surmountable, where the air and water—and maybe Grady—seemed to heal some of Mateo's wounds.

Grady awoke slowly the next morning, his head no longer on the pillow, his arms stretched out on the mattress above his head. He felt a little groggy and light-headed, like he'd taken something to help him sleep or had slept too long. He had no desire to open his eyes to the harsh morning light.

He could feel the warmth of Mateo alongside him, one of Mateo's hands splayed over his stomach beneath the sheet.

He also felt…

Something cold and hard wrapped around his wrists, and he couldn't lift his arms.

He jerked his eyes open and tugged. Something metal clanked against the iron headboard. The handcuffs.

He was cuffed to the bed.

But that wasn't his main concern anymore.

All he could focus on was who sat in a chair facing him at the end of the bed.

Mateo. His upper body, arms, and legs were all tied to the chair, his mouth gagged. His eyes were full of both agony and rage.

"Teo."

The man lying under the sheet beside Grady removed the

hand from his stomach and turned away before Grady got a look at his face. The bed shifted with his weight as he swung his legs over the side and stood, his back to Grady. His hair was buzzed, his shoulders broad and square. He was dressed in camouflage hunting gear.

He turned toward the bed. Half his face was scarred, burned so badly it looked like the flesh had melted and slid an inch or two out of place.

When he spoke, his voice sounded just as damaged as his face, like he'd broken it with his screams.

"Thanks for helping me find him, Grady."

Chapter Eleven

Sergio glared down at Grady and spoke again in that beastly, scratchy voice.

"I appreciate you bringing him to such a remote location."

That voice almost sounded creepier than his words.

Almost.

What was even more alarming was the handgun he held along his right leg, the barrel pointed at the floor. He was idly tapping it against his thigh like it was an umbrella and he was just killing time until the rain started coming down again. His face was so damaged on the right side it was hard to read his expression, but the other side showcased a vile leer that sent a shudder through Grady. Sergio's eyes were dark, and his hair and skin were ashen. He looked like a ghost—a ghost with a score to settle.

"Fuck you!" Grady struggled against the restraints. "I'm not letting you hurt him again."

Sergio laughed. That cold, calculating glare grew beyond disturbing. He tapped, tapped, tapped the gun's barrel against his leg. "What do you think you're gonna do to me?" Then slowly, tauntingly he turned toward Mateo. "I always knew you'd end up back with this loser one day. I knew he meant more to you than you ever made it sound. And since he wasn't hiding from me, he was the one I had followed."

Grady stilled as he processed that. This was his fault. Just like he'd feared, he'd led this guy right to Mateo. He looked toward the end of the bed.

Mateo was staring back at him. His face was drawn with pain and exhaustion. How long had he been tied to that chair while Grady lay there sleeping? With how light-headed Grady had felt when he'd awoken—and the fact that he hadn't heard any sort of struggle around him—Sergio must have injected him with something. Or maybe he'd slipped it into their food. Maybe that was why it had taken him over a day to make his move. The thought of him outside, waiting for the right moment, pissed Grady off something fierce. That anger almost canceled out the fear.

The gag on Mateo was so tight around his mouth it looked painful. Grady struggled against the cuffs again, wrenching and twisting his arms and body, desperately trying to get free.

"Oh, yeah." Sergio stepped toward Mateo. "I think this will work out better than I planned." Another step. "You took everything from me. Taking him from you will be the best revenge." He glanced back over his shoulder at Grady and kept speaking to Mateo. "But first I'm thinking…fucking him while you have to watch will be icing on the cake. Make up for all those times you were thinking of him when you were fucking me."

A muffled, unintelligible series of howls poured out of Mateo from behind the gag as he strained against the ropes.

Curiosity apparently did Sergio in. He reached out and tugged down the gag.

The words spat out of Mateo without delay. "You lay one hand on him, and I swear to you—"

Sergio raised the gun. "Shut up." He made like he was going to return the gag, then evidently thought better of it. "I always knew he was there between us. From day one until you turned me in, he was in my way." He cupped Mateo's cheek and moved his hand in a slow caress along Mateo's jawline. "I could've loved you forever."

Hearing those words, seeing him touching Mateo, spurred Grady into action. Craning his neck, he searched the nightstand for the key to the handcuffs, trying to look without letting on to the asshole.

He spotted the key. Still where Mateo had dropped it earlier.

Grady sat up as best as he could and stretched toward the table, leaning in so his face was close enough he could try to grasp the key between his lips. Thank God the asshole had handcuffed him on that side of the bed. If he could just get another inch closer. He stretched more.

Mateo must've seen what he was up to. He spoke to Sergio, no longer yelling, keeping him distracted.

"I did love you. And you betrayed that."

Grady put everything he had into the stretch, his arm muscles straining with the effort. He was gonna pull something in another minute.

Then he had the key clasped between his teeth. He worked his way back to lying straight on the bed and then shimmied up the mattress toward the headboard, arching until he could get the key between his fingers. He clasped it, pinching as hard as he could so he didn't drop it. He had one shot at this.

He maneuvered the key around until he had it aimed at one side of the cuffs, using the tip to feel for the keyhole, keeping his eye on the asshole's back at the end of the bed.

Mateo spoke again. "You made me a promise that you were done with that life. You lied to me."

"And you lied to *me*. I always thought you didn't tell me his name because you were trying to show me he was in your past, that it was me you wanted. But you never said it because you knew I'd see how much you loved him, and I'd know then that what you felt for me couldn't even come close." Sergio turned his back on him and faced the bed.

Grady hid the key in a closed fist.

The asshole spoke as he moved toward Grady again. "I'm not the liar here. I'm a man of my word, and I'll prove it." He reached for his pants and popped open the top button. The leer on his face this time had something much more sexual to it.

Mateo kept talking, the words coming out in a rush. "How did you find him?"

Sergio looked smug. The fucking asshole was proud of himself. He kept looking at Grady but spoke to Mateo. "You once told me you two played hockey together. I went through a few candid shots of the hockey team at your old school, and it was pretty obvious which one he was. You never looked at me that way." He licked his lips and moved closer to the bed, rubbing himself through his pants. "Then when I saw that message he posted on Facebook, I knew it wouldn't be long."

With his attention focused on Grady's naked torso, Grady took a chance and went back to working with the key above his head, trying to keep his movements small, unseen.

"No worries," Sergio said as he set the gun down on the nightstand. "I'll make this good for you." He took off his shirt, revealing more burns along half his upper body. He crawled onto the bed, his pants still on but open at the front. "It's been a very long time since I've had this pleasure with anyone." He slowly peeled the sheet off Grady's naked lower body.

Mateo screamed obscenities at Sergio's back as he struggled with even more vigor to get free from the chair. Then he yelled promise after promise of what he was going to do to Sergio when he got free, the chair creaking under his thrashing weight.

Sergio slid on top of Grady. His skin was clammy. He felt like dead weight, like a lifeless carcass and not a real, breathing person. "Spread your legs for me."

"Fuck you!" Grady spat the words at him. The key slid into the lock, and it turned. His left hand was free. He fished the cuffs through the headboard so he had both arms loose, then surged up, shoving a surprised Sergio off him. Grady lunged for the gun on the nightstand and fumbled with it for a moment but got a hold of the grip. He spun around. Only...

Sergio was already crouched behind Mateo. He had a second, smaller gun aimed straight at Grady. "Don't even think about it. I'm a much better shot than you."

Okay, he had him with that one. Grady had never held a gun in his hands, let alone fired one.

Sergio continued. "So here's your choice. I'm going to shoot you, then Mateo. Or you drop that gun right now. I'll still kill you, but I'll let him live like I said I would. After all, I'm a man of my word." He snaked a hand around Mateo's throat and jerked him backward. "Right, *Teo*?"

"Don't fucking call me that." Mateo was struggling again— this time both against the restraints and the hand at his throat. Then, as if Sergio's words had really sunk in, he stopped. He stared at Grady, horror etched on his face. Then a stark fearlessness—and confidence—fell over his features.

Without giving it any more thought, Grady understood what Mateo was saying. The way he'd always been able to read him when they were kids.

Mateo was telling him to do it.

Grady gave a slight nod and squeezed the trigger.

Sergio was down in an instant, the gun he'd held skidding across the floor and stopping near the kitchen table. Blood was seeping out the wound in his shoulder while Grady's ears were still ringing from the sound of the shot.

Grady kept the gun aimed at where Sergio lay on the floor and rushed to Mateo's other side. "Are you okay?"

Mateo didn't respond. He was staring at Sergio.

"Teo, are you hurt?"

Nothing.

"Teo!"

He blinked and seemed to regain focus. "I'm fine. Are you okay?"

"Yeah." Grady worked to untie him from the chair, trying to keep the gun steady and locked on Sergio at the same time. When Mateo was free, Grady went for his cell phone and dialed 911. After he hung up, he said, "They're on their way."

Mateo was standing then, staring down at Sergio again. Grady couldn't read that expression on his face. Anger? Rage? Maybe mixed with something like disbelief and relief all at once.

Grady tugged on his arm. "Don't stand so close. And don't you move," he added for Sergio, who had a hand pressed to his shoulder and was glaring up at them.

By the look on his face, he really hadn't thought it would come to this. He'd thought he had won the minute he'd stepped inside the guesthouse. He started to sit up but stopped when Mateo took a step closer.

Mateo held out an open hand to Grady. "Give me the gun."

"No way. He's destroyed your life enough already."

With a slow sweep of his head as if he didn't want to take his eyes off Sergio, Mateo looked Grady's way. "I'm not going to hurt him unless he gives me a reason to. I just need to make sure he doesn't move, that he doesn't get away this time."

Grady trusted Mateo, trusted that he wouldn't take a shot, kill an unarmed man, and ruin their future together. He handed him the gun.

Mateo aimed it at Sergio with decisive conviction, like someone who'd spent a lot of time at a firing range, or someone who'd spent a long time waiting for this moment. "Don't you fucking move one inch."

Grady was glad he'd given him the chance to be the one who kept Sergio lying there until help arrived.

Mateo needed to do this. He needed the closure.

* * * *

Grady shook the sheriff's hand and offered her his thanks again. Then he did the same with Riley, only his brother ignored the offered hand and pulled him into a hug.

"I'm proud of you, little brother."

Grady laughed. It felt good to let out some of the tension. "You're *my* little brother, Riley."

"Nah. I don't think so." Riley pulled back, a look of feigned contemplation on his face. "All the evidence points to the contrary. I mean, you've just now landed yourself your first boyfriend. That sounds pretty young to me." He gave him a wink, then walked off with the sheriff, calling back, "I'll come by and pick you guys up in the morning."

Grady and Mateo weren't done with the interviews yet. No one was questioning their side of the story, not once they saw who he'd shot, but he and Mateo would have to go into the station the next day and finish giving their statements, then talk to the local feds. It wouldn't be over for a while.

But oddly, it felt finished.

He hoped it did for Mateo too.

And yet it also felt like a brand-new start. Like Grady's life was just getting going.

He watched Riley and the sheriff drive off down the dirt driveway, like he'd watched the ambulance leave with Sergio an hour earlier. When the cars were out of sight through the trees, he turned and headed for the water's edge.

Mateo was sitting in the sand, looking out over the lake again. He'd been obsessed with the water since he'd gotten there. Perhaps it gave him a peace that nothing else ever could—or would.

Grady sat beside him and joined him in watching a pair of swans gracefully slice through the water's surface, leaving a dance of ripples in their wake.

Maybe Mateo wasn't the only one who found the lake peaceful, healing.

Grady leaned in and bumped shoulders with him. "Please tell me I didn't just shoot a guy you still love."

Mateo sharply looked his way. "Are you serious?"

He wasn't. Not really. But a part of him wanted to hear it.

As if reading his thoughts, Mateo said, "You just shot a psychotic asshole who was about to kill the man I love."

They held the gaze for a long moment. Grady was the first to look away, trying to find the pair of swans again, but they were gone. He said, "I love you too." The next words were nearly impossible to say, but he had to. "I've been thinking, though... You've been held prisoner in your own life long enough. So I'm going to drop you back off at home. And I'm going to leave you alone. When—and if—you want to see me again, that'll be your call. You know how I feel. You know I'm ready for this."

Out of the corner of his eye, he could see Mateo watching him for a few more seconds, and then he too went back to focusing on the water. "What if I tell you it feels like I already am home?" There was a new calmness to him that was very different from the man he'd been when they'd arrived at the lake, and yet also different from the man he'd been back in school.

His trust issues might have started out because of Grady, but in the end they were mostly about Sergio. Maybe now that the asshole was in custody, everything Mateo had been going through really did feel finished for him. Maybe letting Grady in also had something to do with that.

But...

"Teo, you said I hurt you more than he did."

Mateo shook his head. "That's not true. I was just angry."

"But maybe I did. Deep down. Maybe the scars I left on you were worse than his."

"No, they weren't. Because I knew you loved me. I knew it with everything I was. Even if you didn't want to see it. And knowing that, remembering that...gave me hope, gave me a possible future to fight for." Mateo paused, then spoke again with certainty. "I don't want to spend another day without you."

Grady let the relief rush out of him through a wide, dopey grin, not giving a damn what he looked like. He was done hiding what he felt, done pretending anything. "Then you forgive me?"

Mateo didn't answer right away, just kept scanning the surface of the water, like he too was looking for those lost swans. Then he said, "I'm not sure you need forgiving, but yeah, I do. Can you forgive me?"

"For what?"

"For not understanding you weren't ready six years ago. I shouldn't have pushed you like that. It was too soon, all too new for both of us."

"I guess it was." Grady bumped shoulders with him again. "Do you believe I'm ready now?"

Mateo smiled, a match to Grady's stupid grin. "Yeah."

They looked at each other, and that understanding passed between them again.

Mateo faced the water once more. "Can we stay here for a little while longer?"

"Sure. However long you want."

Without looking Grady's way, he asked, "How about forever?" Then he turned to him again, and for the first time since they'd gotten to the lake, those dark eyes had a peaceful serenity to them. "Does forever work for you?"

Grady moved in behind him, sliding a leg on either side of his. "Yeah, that works."

Mateo settled back, and Grady wrapped both arms around him. Together they watched the two swans float out from farther down shore where they'd been hiding in a stretch of cattail stalks. The pair glided across the surface of the lake in a tranquil, harmonious rhythm.

Two destined souls moving and living and loving together as one, and both stronger because of that.

Sample Chapters from

HOW TO SAVE A LIFE by Sloan Parker

PROLOGUE

"You're mine now."

The eerie whispered voice from behind him urged Seth Fisher into action. He scrambled onto his hands and knees and lunged for the nightstand. If he could just reach a weapon from the table, the phone or a lamp—

The man wrapped his hands around Seth's ankles and tugged him backward. Seth surged forward again with everything he had, ignoring the scrape and burn of the carpet on his bare elbows and knees. He clutched the leg of the nightstand in both hands and added several hard, backward kicks, desperately trying to connect with the face of the creep behind him.

The kicking wasn't working. He made contact with the empty air more than the man. Too late now to get in any more good kicks. The creep's weight pressed down on Seth. Heavy, warm breaths hit the skin at the back of his ear.

"Fighting with me won't stop the inevitable."

Oddly, that time the whispered voice didn't sound as threatening as the words implied.

This guy was having fun.

Fuck you, asshole. Seth wasn't about to give up because this guy told him to.

He opened his mouth to scream, and a hand cut off the sound.

Not just a hand. A moist cloth covered Seth's mouth and nose. He squirmed harder, struggled to get leverage with his knees, but he couldn't move an inch.

His head spun, and his grip on the leg of the nightstand relaxed. He clawed at the wood, struggling to grab hold again.

Instead he watched with disbelief as his hands let go. The edges of his vision darkened. The last thing he saw was the creep's large hands wrapping around his own and pulling them away from the nightstand.

And the last thought he had was he really should've listened to his friend Toby. He never should've come to the Haven.

The next time Seth Fisher awoke, he lay naked on an oversize pillow on the floor of a tiny, locked metal cage with nothing to do but wait for the man who'd taken him to return.

Or for someone else to find him.

Chapter One

Stupid leather pants.

Kevin Price stood in the aisle of the crowded downtown bus and tried not to draw attention to himself.

Hard to do while attempting to get the most ridiculous, tightest pants known to man out of the crack of his ass.

Why the hell had he listened to Myles about what to wear?

"It's a sex club. You gotta look sexy."

Asshole.

Why would anyone wear pants like this?

To get laid.

If he could remember when he'd last had sex, he might've contemplated that longer.

The bus neared Kevin's stop. *Thank God.* He tugged on the legs of the pants and took a step forward. The elderly woman he'd given his seat to ten minutes earlier halted her knitting and gripped his wrist with a cold, bony hand.

"You don't want to get off here." Her grip tightened as she leaned in and hissed her next words in a low whisper. "It's not safe."

Could the universe please help him out?

Like walking into a gay sex club wasn't hard enough.

He smiled down at her and gave her hand a pat. "I'll be all right." When she didn't let go, he tried another smile and pat.

She had her gaze locked on his, but it was as if she didn't see him. Like she was in a trance. Then she squinted. The whites of her eyes grew smaller until there was nothing left but the gray of the irises. "You can't hide from him. He'll find you there. He'll find you anywhere."

Why did he always attract the weirdest people wherever he went?

"Okay," he said. "Thanks for the tip."

Finally she released him. He hurried away before he missed his stop, or before the creepy old woman gave him another obscure prediction. His skin was still crawling from that first one.

She was right, though. It wasn't safe where he was headed. Three missing young men. Another beaten. And no one was doing anything to find out why—or to stop it.

Until now.

The bus lurched forward and then came to a sudden stop. Kevin rushed the rest of the way to the front. *Great.* The leather pants now rode even higher up his ass. He stepped onto the curb, and the stifling heat slammed into him, knocking the breath from his chest. The sun had been down for hours, and still the heat hung over the city, draining the life and motivation from everyone.

Well, almost everyone.

He blew a strand of hair out of his eyes and tugged at the leather again.

No matter what, he had no intention of giving up on his plans. He'd never forgive himself if he walked away before he got to the truth and kept someone else from getting hurt—or worse.

He turned and headed north into the darkness of the old downtown factory district, thankful the crappy streetlamps and shadows of night would help cover the waddle in his stride as he tried to work the leather out of his ass with each step.

He took in the details of his surroundings. The unending cracks in the sidewalk, the smell of garbage and urine from the deserted alley, the shuffle of the homeless man's steps across the street.

The bleak locale had to be intentional. Only men serious about what they wanted would come to this neighborhood, would go out of their way to reach the Haven, a membership-only club where gay men could find—according to the club's

Web site—"a safe and sane environment where every fantasy comes true."

Fantasies? Kevin had rolled his eyes when he'd read that part. No one actually wanted their fantasies to come true. Did they?

What kind of people paid to go somewhere to fuck strangers?

Yet the mere thought of what he might see inside the club had his body thrumming with excitement, his blood heading south.

Stupid. Fucking. Dick. The traitorous thing never did listen to him.

He wiped the sweat beading at the nape of his neck. It was hot as hell walking the streets during the worst heat wave the city had seen in years. Of course, wearing the long-sleeve shirt and too-tight leather pants didn't help. The sweat now dripped down the crack of his ass, making him even more aware he'd skipped underwear since he hadn't been certain he could fit them on underneath.

He was going to kill Myles.

Like Kevin would look sexy walking in there with the stupid pants up his ass, his stomach twisted in knots, and his brain warring with his dick.

If only he hadn't made himself one promise years ago.

He'd fucked up, and it had cost him too much. That was all he needed to remember.

That, and the fact that he was not gay.

Not gay. Not gay. Not gay.

Another few strides, another run-down building, and he neared a five-story brick structure. The place had the same exterior as the abandoned buildings surrounding it, with graffiti and chipped, aging bricks. No sign with flashing red neon letters announcing *hot man-on-man action here*. No sign of any kind.

Kevin made his way toward the building's front door. His phone rang, and his steps faltered as he shoved his hand into the front pocket of the tight-as-hell pants without thinking of the consequences. He did a little shimmy with his hips, but his hand wouldn't budge.

He couldn't walk into a swanky, underground sex club with one hand stuck inside his pants. He'd probably look like he was trying to grope himself as soon as he stepped inside. He might as well paint a sign on his forehead: *Gay virgin here. First night in a gay bar.*

Well, not his first, but pretty damn close.

He gave another tug and breathed a sigh of relief when both his hand and the phone slid out. The movement, however, sent him tripping over a raised crack in the sidewalk. He flung forward, smacking his palm on the brick wall, just stopping his face from the same outcome.

A cab pulled up to the front of the club. Kevin leaned his shoulder against the brick and tried to appear casual, like he hadn't just tripped over practically nothing.

Smooth. He was so not going to fit in at the Haven. He couldn't even walk inside without making a fool of himself.

His phone rang again, and he checked the display. Perfect timing.

Guys walking into a sex club did not get calls from their mommies.

She probably just wanted to ask for the twentieth time if he planned to get back with Sondra. He hit the button to send the call to his voice mail.

A burly guy wearing a leather vest and pants got out of the cab and went to the Haven's front door. Two more men passed by Kevin.

No way they had missed his stellar trip into the brick. Both men gave him a sidelong glance as they entered. One winked at him.

Another man on foot appeared from around the far corner of the building. A tall, dark figure slinking toward him from out of the shadows. Kevin set his phone to vibrate and stashed it in his pocket, twisting his hips to get his hand out. The action was getting easier. Maybe the leather was stretching and he'd be able to get out of the pants later without anyone's assistance.

He got out the key card he'd received the day before and

took a step closer to the door. His phone vibrated in his pocket. His mom had probably gotten cut off by his voice mail and she was calling to leave part two. She had the worst timing. She always called him right as he was about to get laid.

That had him frozen in place with his hand on the club's door handle. No way would he be getting laid tonight. Not in *there*.

He threw open the door, made it one step inside, and froze again.

He'd been in the Haven the previous day for an interview, but that had been an hour before they'd opened for the night. The brief tour of the posh club hadn't prepared him for the live show.

Men were everywhere. Dancing. Talking. Kissing. Grinding body against body. Practically fucking in the lounge chairs and on the dance floor while more men filled the dining room, eating their meals like they dined in any other upscale restaurant in the city.

The music was slower than he expected, softer. The lighting subtle. Not the dark corners, flashing strobe lights, and sea of strung out, desperate losers he'd pictured.

"Excuse me," came a deep voice from behind him.

Kevin spun around. The dark-haired man from outside had stopped in the club's doorway, staring down at him. He stood over half a foot taller, wearing jeans and a snug black T-shirt that showed off every firm muscle and looked both casual and dressy at the same time. Or maybe it was the man underneath. Short dark hair, slicked back. A touch of gray at his temples. He reminded Kevin of a vampire. Sleek, sophisticated, ready to attack.

A sexy-assed vampire with a concentrated stare. Serious. Beautiful.

Was it offensive to call a man beautiful?

Or to call him a vampire?

"You in or out?" the guy asked in a low voice that gave credence to the vampire imagery.

Kevin could not stop staring. He also couldn't get his jaw to cooperate. He just stood there with his mouth hanging open.

Gay virgin here.

Yeah, he was doing a hell of a job blending in.

The guy hadn't looked away yet. He raised his eyebrows and pointed behind Kevin. "There's the dining room. That's for talking and eating." He pointed to his right. "There's the bar. That's for drinking and dancing." He gestured in the opposite direction. "There's the lounge. That's mostly for making out." He leaned closer and pointed over Kevin's shoulder to the far side of the first floor, his breath brushing Kevin's earlobe as he said, "There's the stairs. That's where you head up to the rooms for more than making out." He pulled back. "Pick your poison."

Poison? Interesting choice of words. Wasn't the guy a member? Didn't he enjoy coming here?

Kevin clamped his mouth shut and breathed deep through his nose. Not a good idea. The guy smelled amazing. All male. Deeper, richer than any cologne he'd ever purchased. Kevin squeezed his eyes shut, and his body responded to the lust thundering through him.

Not now.

He opened his eyes.

The dark-haired man waited a moment, smirked, then stepped around him and walked off.

Kevin ran a hand down his chest, smoothing his shirt. He finally got moving and rushed for the bar. Everyone watching him cross the room had to know exactly what state his body was in.

Stupid, stupid pants.

How had he ended up here?

For years now he'd forced himself to stop checking out the porn sites. To stay clear of the locker room at the gym. To make a weekly date with Sondra even if work kept him busy.

He'd done all he could to forget that night. To move on.

Five minutes inside the Haven, one sexy-as-fuck older man, and that was all blown to hell. He was in serious trouble.

Kevin picked up the pace, then caught a glimpse of Vampire Guy's ass as the man walked toward the back of the club. Kevin wanted to grab that ass in his hands and sink his mouth over the guy's dick.

Oh God.
He turned away.
Not gay?
Right. Nice try.

Chapter Two

Walter Simon headed up the flight of stairs and noted the hush of the crowd behind him. Then the whispers started. Even the thumping beat of the music from the bar didn't mask the muffled mentions of his name as he made his way up.

His visits to the Haven had been anything but regular in recent years, and yet it was always the same thing.

Every instinct told him to turn and stare them down, keep his back to the wall and his eyes on the crowd.

He would always be a cop. Always be on duty. No matter how long ago he'd turned in his badge.

He sighed and kept on climbing.

Vargas stood waiting for him at the top of the staircase. He held out a hand. "Simon."

They'd been friends for as long as Vargas had owned the club, and in all that time they'd never called each other by their first names.

"Thanks for coming right over."

They shook as Walter said, "Not a problem. Did you keep everyone out of the room?"

"Yeah. No one else is going in there until you say so."

"No problems with the new security system?" Walter's company had done the installation.

"Seems to be working fine, despite what's been going on." Vargas swept his arm through the air like everything around him had been turning to shit.

"The extra cameras we put up last week should help."

"I hope so." Vargas's phone rang. He checked the display. "Hang on for a minute? I've got to take this."

Walter gave a nod, and Vargas went to the reservation desk situated at the top of the stairs to answer his call.

Despite how concerned Vargas had sounded on the phone earlier when he'd called Walter, he didn't look it. He appeared as unruffled and confident as always, even with the dress shirt open at the top two buttons and the tie he usually wore long gone.

Everyone said the two of them could be brothers. Same height, same dark hair, although Vargas didn't have the gray running through his, and Walter didn't have the tattooed phrases hidden under his shirt that Vargas had.

They'd worked out at the gym together enough times over the years that he knew it'd be a toss-up if the two of them ever had to settle a disagreement with their fists. As it was, they'd likely kill themselves one day trying to outdo the other on the weight bench or the track.

The years after forty only intensified that drive. For both men.

Walter turned and scanned the crowd on the first floor below, taking note of who he recognized, who was new, who looked like they'd come for reasons other than a hookup.

Walking toward a table in the bar was the man he'd spoken to at the entrance. Still looking shocked, with a curious, nervous scan of his eyes. This guy was definitely hiding something. He was also so far in the closet he'd need a road map and a compass to find his way out.

The young man fumbled with a chair and plopped into the seat, all while he stared at the crowd of dancing men in the bar.

He had wavy—or more accurately, disheveled—light brown hair, a little too long for the style, like he only bothered to get it cut when the hair got to the point where it hung in his eyes. Or maybe not even then, judging by the way he blew the strands from his face. An adorable move.

Wait. When had Walter last found anyone adorable? Had he ever?

The leather pants had probably never been worn before and were at least a size too small. The long-sleeve blue dress shirt was one too big. More fabric covered the young man's body than was typical for the Haven. The dining room could be reserved at dinner, but the bar leaned more to the casual side, shirts falling off as the night went on.

This guy was modest. Uncomfortable, even.

He shifted in his seat and yanked on his pant legs with both hands.

Walter smirked, barely holding back the laugh. He stilled the reaction and forced down a stiff swallow. He was done with the casual thing, and if he hooked up with a guy that young, it could never be more than a one-night stand. By the time a guy like that turned forty, Walter would be storing his teeth in a cup at night and using one of those motorized carts at the grocery store to pick up his adult diapers.

He gave up on the crowd as soon as Vargas returned. He couldn't stop from asking the question, though. "Who's that guy sitting alone in the bar? The one in the leather pants?"

"Kevin Dennison. He's a paralegal at a law firm. You know him?"

"No. Just getting the lay of the land, checking out who's here."

"You ready to head up?" Vargas gestured to the elevator.

The Haven had five stories. The first floor held the public areas. The other floors had the private rooms, most equipped like a hotel. The reservation desk sat at the top of the stairs on the second floor and was visible to the dining room and bar below. An elevator was located on the first floor to the right of the main staircase for those who'd already reserved a room where they'd spend the rest of the night. Or a half hour. Whatever they preferred.

Vargas hit the fourth-floor button. "Here's Seth Fisher's info." He handed over a thin folder.

A single sheet of paper with a photocopy of a driver's license lay inside. "This is his file?"

"No." Vargas pointed at the paper. "That's what I'm giving you of his file. I'm not about to violate my member's privacy any more than I have to. You only get what you absolutely need."

That's one of the reasons Walter liked Vargas. The man was

honest and trustworthy. And he genuinely gave a shit. About his friends. About the club's members. About honor and integrity. There weren't many men like him around these days.

Didn't that thought make Walter feel old?

He examined the copy of the license. At least he had a name, Seth Fisher, and an address.

"He's twenty-five," Vargas said. "As you can see from his picture, he looks younger than that. Been a member for a year."

The photocopied picture of Seth was dark but clear enough. He looked like…

"Yeah," Vargas said in a low voice. "I thought so too."

Walter glanced up, and Vargas added, "They kept running his picture in the paper."

Right. Five years was a long time to remember one kid's face, but the story had been in the news for weeks after the shooting. Walter carefully folded the photocopy, slipped it into his pocket, and gave Vargas back the empty folder.

The elevator chimed, and the doors opened.

"If this is too much—"

Walter held up a hand. "No. I'm fine." He followed Vargas into the hall. "So I gather from what you said earlier there have been more missing items?"

"Yeah. Nothing major. Linens, towels, liquor. Like the others. Some shipments messed up too." He hesitated. "Maybe that's what's got me thinking this is more than it looks like."

Walter laid a hand on his shoulder and stopped him from continuing down the hall. "You okay?"

Vargas huffed out a laugh. "I was hoping this would be over by now. That I'd find out the thefts were the work of an employee. Then I could fire his ass and get back to my normal, boring routine."

Funny a guy who owned a sex club thought his life was boring. Or normal.

It probably was. Walter had seen a lot of nasty shit during his years on the force. Most people didn't know how abnormal the world could be.

He tipped his head, indicating farther down the hall. "This is more serious?"

"I'm no cop, but yeah, I think so."

"Okay. Let's take a look."

They walked again. Vargas stopped at the third door from the end of the long hall and swiped a key card.

"Wait." Walter gestured for him to hold back. He stepped in first and scanned the room.

A double bed, unmade. Sheets and bedspread rumpled, half on the foot of the bed, half on the floor. He crossed to the opposite side of the room, surveying the space from a different angle.

Two lamps, one on each nightstand. The far lamp had a crack from the top of the shade to the bottom and sat close to the back edge of the table. One side of the nightstand was farther away from the wall than the other.

He crouched and examined under the bed. Nothing. He straightened and moved to the bar in the corner. It was made of solid wood, sturdy. He checked under there as well. The leg closest to the door was shifted backward from its usual indent in the carpet, the indent still perfectly pressed in. A recent move.

Vargas spoke. "Two guys came in here after we first opened and found it like this. Same as the other rooms last month, but…"

Walter stood and kept looking over the space. "What?"

"I had a bad feeling this time. That it was more than someone sneaking in here for a quickie. Last night only one person came upstairs without stopping at the desk. Seth Fisher." Vargas turned his head and stared through the room's open door to the empty hall. "He never came down or scanned his ID on his way out. I haven't been able to get a hold of him since." He gave up on the door and focused on Walter again. "If he was in this room, something happened to him, didn't it?"

"Maybe." Walter pointed to the bar. "This was pushed back. One side of the nightstand was dragged three inches. The lamp fell over, and the shade was crushed in, but someone popped it back out. Those all indicate a struggle someone tried to clean up after, but a few details were missed." He pointed to the bed. "Employees hanging out in the rooms before or after hours wouldn't leave the bed unmade. They'd try to make the room look as it did before they entered. Whoever was in here wanted to clean up the part that indicated a struggle but didn't care if you knew someone had been in the room."

"Which means?"

"He wanted you to think it's about sex. Maybe the cleaning crew would come in and take care of things, unaware the room hadn't been reserved. Then no one would know his real reason for being here."

Vargas looked ill. He drew in a deep breath. "If I call the cops with all that, they'll laugh their asses off and hang up on me, won't they?"

"Probably. They'll just say Seth could've been here to meet an employee who helped him sneak out after hours. They'll file a report, at most. Maybe knock on the kid's door. There's not enough here to suggest foul play, not at a sex club."

Vargas shook his head. "They won't even look for him." He stormed across the room and slammed the door shut, keeping his palm flattened to the door. "I want to know what's going on in my club." He held his hand against the surface of the door for a moment more, then faced Walter.

Whether it was instinct or his old training resurfacing, Walter knew something was wrong here. Very wrong. He couldn't walk away without knowing what had happened to Seth Fisher—without knowing if he was okay.

"I'll find him."

ABOUT THE AUTHOR

Sloan Parker writes passionate, dramatic stories about two men (or more) falling in love. She enjoys writing in the fictional world because in fiction you can be anything, do anything— even fall in love for the first time over and over again. Sloan lives in Ohio with her partner and their neurotic cats. Her greatest moments in life are spent with her family, her friends, and her characters.

To contact Sloan, find out about her other books that are available for purchase, and read free stories, visit: www.sloanparker.com. If you'd like to be notified of new releases and get exclusive sneak peeks, be sure to sign up to receive Sloan Parker's newsletter via her website.

OTHER TITLES BY SLOAN PARKER

MORE series
More (More Book 1)
More Than Most (More Book 2)

THE HAVEN series
How to Save a Life (The Haven Book 1)

Single Titles
Breathe
Take Me Home
More Than Just a Good Book
Something to Believe In
Friends and Lovers
The Break-In
Swept Away
A Lesson in Truth